THE GARLAND GIRL

It was a stranger who had begun the process of recovery, from the deaths of her father and boyfriend, that enabled Leila Garland to face the world again. A stranger called Matt Parnell—who was to have more impact on her life than she knew . . .

THE GARLAND GIRL

BY

LIZA MANNING

MILLS & BOON LIMITED
15–16 BROOK'S MEWS
LONDON W1A 1DR

*First published in Great Britain 1985
by Mills & Boon Limited*

© Liza Manning 1985

*Australian copyright 1985
Philippine copyright 1985
This edition 1985*

ISBN 0 263 75206 2

*Set in Monophoto Times 10 on 10 pt.
01–1185   63993*

*Made and printed in Great Britain by
Richard Clay (The Chaucer Press) Ltd,
Bungay, Suffolk*

CHAPTER ONE

SHE was a good-looking girl on holiday in Hawaii. One of the multitudes peopling the dazzling beaches, the crowded streets and the expensive nightclubs. They were there in every conceivable shape and size, every degree of sun-tan, almost nude in their tiny bikinis.

Her name was Leila Garland. That much they knew at the hotel, where to the American and Japanese guests she was something of a mystery. The Hawaiian muu-muus she wore down to the beach covered bikinis every bit as brief as any to be seen in the Islands. Her figure was superb, her tan even and well established; she had the easy assurance of someone used to an expensive lifestyle, but she made no attempt to glamorise herself, wore little make-up, didn't dress up in the evenings. Her honey-coloured hair was bleached by the sun into pale gold streaks and she wore it tied back out of the way, or sometimes piled up loosely on top. She was so quiet and understated in a place where everyone was busy enjoying themselves that she attracted more attention than the noisiest extrovert. And she was always alone.

It was her eyes and her manner which kept off the men. Brown eyes, large and long-lashed, which could have been warm with laughter and easy promise; instead they were careful, cool, and could turn positively glacial if one of the bronzed young men tried to insist on making her acquaintance.

It was known that she was English. Yes, agreed the Americans reluctantly, being English could account for her coolness, her reserve, and after a few days they left her alone—there were plenty of other girls available. She sat uninterrupted at her table for one; made her silent trips to the beaches alone; watched the great glass-green breakers of the Pacific alone. She was thought to be cold, polite, a bit odd. So they said: 'Let her get on with it.'

5

It was a solidly built fellow from Oregon who first recognised her. 'Hey,' he said, nudging his neighbour. 'That classy little piece on her own, the one with blonde hair and the black bikini. She's Pearson's girl, ain't she? Lance Pearson. You recall him—one of the big-time surfers. They were always together. Saw them back home when he gave those demonstrations.'

The eyes of the man next to him remained slitted behind dark glasses. It was hot and he was wondering whether to go on a trip round Pearl Harbor. 'So?'

'So that's why she's alone,' said the man from Oregon, wriggling with pleasure. He liked imparting information and he could see two middle-aged women hovering nearby so as not to miss what came next. 'Pearson's dead. Drowned. Yeah, drowned in the big surf in Australia. No wonder she don't look too happy.'

In no time at all everyone in the hotel knew that Leila had been Lance Pearson's girl. The men eyed her with renewed curiosity, the women with a touch of envy and some sympathy. After all, it was said she'd kept Pearson, that he'd lived on her money. Of course, he'd been quite a spectacular guy, a wonderful physique and as handsome as they come, but just look at her now. It hadn't done her much good, had it?

The subject of these speculations would have been amazed to know of the interest she aroused. She was hardly aware of giving amorous males the brush-off, of being cool and reserved. Her mind was occupied with the self-imposed task of reorganising her life and fighting off the ever-present remorse which weighed her down.

It had taken all her courage to return to Hawaii, a tropical playground with an all-the-year season and enough good humour to sicken anyone not in the mood for it. Just one thing had brought her back; the need to straighten out her life from its present chaos in the place where she had once been happy.

Hawaii had been the setting for those early heart-stopping weeks with Lance. Their first visit ten months ago had come near to perfection. They had stayed in the busy tourist area of Waikiki Beach, travelling each day to the north of the island for the surfing. It had been the time of that first magnetic attraction between them, the time when she fell deeper in love as each day passed; before she knew that he had to be constantly and expensively on the move in search of the big surf, and long before she realised that there was no future for them together.

It seemed strange that she, who loved silent, uninhabited countryside, who preferred beaches that were deserted in early spring or autumn, should have been so captivated by the islands on that first visit. Even now, ten months older and a century more experienced, she still liked to see the Polynesian beachboys on Waikiki with their surf-boards at the ready for pupils, just as it still delighted her to be presented with the traditional *lei*—the garland of flowers—when she stepped from the plane at Honolulu.

But this time it was different. Too much had happened. She had gone through too much. If ever she was to get back to normal she must start a new life; bid a last farewell of the spirit to the man who had monopolised her in life and continued to do so in death.

Two weeks of her stay had gone past before she began to pay any real attention to her surroundings. One morning it occurred to her that the desk clerk was perhaps rather reserved for an islander. She summoned a hesitant smile and was rewarded by a warm-hearted Polynesian beam. So—it was her. They must have found her stiff and unapproachable, and maybe a few other things as well.

She walked to the lift, conscious of complete exhaustion. Tension had robbed her of sleep, taken her appetite, painted shadows beneath her eyes. Life seemed no easier but imperceptibly she started to relax. Perhaps returning to Hawaii hadn't been a mistake after all.

She continued to waken at daybreak, and savouring the coolness, would slip out before the staff were on duty to wander the beaches in solitude. Sometimes she'd seen a man wind-surfing in a quiet lagoon behind the headland, expertly handling his graceful red-sailed board, using the breeze to full advantage. But Leila noticed him because he, too, was always alone.

One morning just before dawn she sat and gazed silently over the lagoon, the palms waving lazily above her, the sand stained pink with the reflection of the sky. The man was out there again in the rosy half-light. His sails looked deep purple, his body black, the sea wine-red, and idly she tried to recall how often she'd seen him at that hour.

It was very quiet, turning her thoughts back remorselessly to her life with Lance. There had always been noise then—the endless crash of the surf, the knowledgeable chat of the surfing fraternity, the revving of cars, the blare of discos. Thoughtfully, chin on her hands, she watched the sail-board skimming silently over the lagoon.

And then the sun came up, triumphantly gold in an apricot sky streaked with the last remnants of cloud. Everything assumed its daytime colouring; silver sand, blue-green water, lush emerald vegetation.

She could see the man quite clearly now. Dark, broad, assured; his brown legs braced against the pull from the sail. He looked mature, solid, and once again she acknowledged a contrast with Lance; this time with his golden leanness, his extreme youth. Was this to be the next phase—comparing everyone and everything with Lance and their life together?

Then the man sailed into the shallows, the red sail dropping to the water as he made for the beach, dragging the board behind him. At once Leila slipped away through the flowering shrubs, but a little of the scene's tranquillity stayed with her, bringing its own small measure of comfort.

Next morning she slept much later than usual. For once she felt hungry, and rang for a hearty breakfast in her room. As she waited for it she showered and found herself viewing the coming day with a tinge of pleasure, smiling slightly when she saw her reflection in the bathroom mirror. She was feeling more alive and it showed. Her deep gold skin had regained some of its former lustre; the shadows beneath her eyes were surely fading; even her thick fair hair swung with renewed life. She ate breakfast on her balcony in the sunshine.

Perhaps today she would go shopping; behave like a tourist.

That evening the other guests watched the Garland girl. She seemed more relaxed, almost approachable. Two young Texans offered to take her on a tour of the Honolulu night spots, and were smilingly refused. Then Leila walked the moonlit beach; alone again with her thoughts.

She didn't know it, but there was more spring to her step, the turn of her head was more alert, the very way she held herself showed a little more vitality. She had wakened early once more, but this time after a sound sleep, and without making any conscious decision to do so found herself walking towards the headland. It was only half-light again, with the strange pinkish glow playing tricks with the colours, and she looked out curiously to see if the same man was there on his sailboard.

The breeze was fresh, and little white-topped waves smacked each other briskly across the lagoon. With a sick jolt of the heart she saw the board with its sails flapping limply on the dark water. She raised a wrist to her lips and bit on it silently, the newfound serenity deserting her. The man was nowhere in sight. There seemed to her to be an ominous silence over the lagoon, a deadly message in the deserted sail-board.

In seconds she was running barefoot down the beach, her feet sinking into the soft sand with nightmarish lack of progress. Her panicking mind saw the sheltered lagoon as part of the ocean itself with its great curling breakers.

She didn't know she screamed, that tears coursed down her cheeks, that she splashed thigh-deep into the water, frenziedly searching. She slipped and almost went under. The salt taste was on her lips, her mouth stretched wide as she gulped air. Her chest hurt. She couldn't breathe.

Strong arms grabbed her from behind even as she found the breath to sob aloud. She felt warm hands on her rib cage through the wet cotton of her muu-muu, then she was whisked up from the water and dumped on dry sand a few yards from the water's edge.

'Stay there!' instructed a man's voice, and she opened her eyes to see the man's back as he dragged the board and sails out of the water. He pulled it clear, walked to a group of rocks, picked up a towel and came back to where she waited, weak with relief.

Making no attempt to see if she wore anything under it he undid the colourful length of cotton and tossed it aside in a sodden heap. Then he wrapped the towel round her and rubbed briskly, finally lifting the damp, honey-coloured hair out of the way while he dried her shoulders.

He wrapped the towel firmly round her, tucking in the end like a sarong, and covering her bare breasts and lacy briefs. Next he calmly strode off to fetch her sandals. He came back to face her, but slowly, almost as if he was deliberately giving her time to calm down.

'Now,' he said. 'What was all that about?'

He was English. She eyed him in embarrassment. The hectic whirl of the last couple of minutes, her excruciating panic, the hard arms around her middle, the brisk towelling. It all seemed utterly mad. She stared at him silently as the painful thudding of her heart slowed, and in those few seconds the beach became bright with the first rays of the sun.

She could see he was an impressive physical specimen, with a broad chest and long, well-muscled legs. His torso and limbs were patterned with the distinctive hair growth of the mature, dark-haired male. His eyes, observing her with wary concern, were a clear, cool grey; the face lean with a high-bridged nose and assertive chin. He looked tough, a no-nonsense sort of man, used to having his own way and no doubt wondering why he'd been landed with a hysterical woman.

He waited for a reply, neither frowning nor smiling, but with the black eyebrows raised and one corner of his mouth slanting upwards. It was, she saw, an extremely beautiful mouth to be set in such a tough, well-used sort of face. The lips, pale against the tan, were smooth and shapely above a jaw dark with beard growth.

All this registered as they faced each other on the silver sand, with the last remnants of night clearing from the sky above them. 'I—I couldn't see you,' she said, weakly.

Still he waited. She wiped tear stains from her cheeks with her fingers. 'You must think me very foolish,' she said hesitantly. 'I had the idea that—that you were drowning.' Wearily she waited for his reaction. If he laughed she would die.

Something changed in the depths of the grey eyes. 'So you decided to rescue me?' His voice was perfectly serious.

'I—I got a bit worked up,' she said with massive understatement. That was as much as she was going to explain.

He nodded, as if strange females screamed and leapt into the water looking for him every morning of his life. 'Well,' he pointed out mildly, 'I wasn't far away, you know. I saw you coming and ran for cover and my swimming trunks behind those rocks. Wind-surfing in the buff is a good sensation, but not with an audience.'

She was intrigued enough to forget her own reactions for a moment. 'I did think I might see you,' she admitted. 'I've seen you once or twice before at daybreak. But I had no intention of watching you in the nude.'

He nodded again. 'I know. Come on, you need some hot coffee. Over there, the white beach-house with the red tulip tree.' He left the sail-board where it was and held out a big hand, obviously expecting to hold hers. Leila ignored it and walked at his side, one hand keeping the towel in place, the other carrying her sandals and muu-muu.

The beach-house was large and well built, similar to hundreds in the Islands; white-walled, the windows set back under an arched verandah, and the garden hedged with flowering shrubs to keep out the sand.

The man leapt up the steps and opened the door, turning to see that she followed. But Leila had travelled the world and wasn't a complete idiot. She was naked except for her damp briefs and this man's towel. She didn't know him from Adam, but he was expecting her to go into his house on a deserted beach, literally at the crack of dawn. With a small sigh she stood quite still, looking up as he waited for her at the top of the steps. Then either reaction or uneasiness made her shiver.

'Come on,' he said impatiently. 'I'm offering hot coffee, not hot passion. I don't attack overwrought young women whose names I don't even know. I'm Matt Parnell—thirty-six years old and English. This house belongs to a friend of mine.'

Slowly she went up the steps. Instinct reassured her. He was genuine, he was—reliable. 'I'm Leila Garland,' she said quietly, and walked past him into the house. She didn't see his expression as he followed her. It held surprise, curiosity, and what could have been pity.

He opened the door of a bedroom and waved her inside. 'Look around, there should be something that will fit you in one of the cupboards. Take what you need. I'll put the coffee on.'

The feeling of exhaustion was upon her again. With an effort she resisted the temptation to sink, damp towel and all, on to the big double bed. Wide windows looked out over the top of blossom-laden frangipani to the silver sands stretching into the distance. Hundreds of yards away, looking puppet-like and silent, two young children were throwing a ball to each other.

The room was spacious and well-furnished, but with an unlived-in look and a fine layer of sandy dust on the tiled floor. The present occupant was hardly the type to run around with a duster, she thought.

Feeling like an intruder she opened the wardrobe and found a woman's shorts. They were too big for her round the waist but she pulled them in with a narrow belt and then picked out a man's shirt, luridly Hawaiian, which came right down over her bottom. Not exactly elegant, but at least dry. Still shivering, she rolled her wet briefs and muu-muu together, slipped on her sandals, picked up the big towel and went to find Matt Parnell.

She followed the smell of coffee and found him in the large square kitchen. He had substituted denim shorts for his wet trunks, and covered up the broad hairy chest with a neatly checked sports shirt. He looked calm and relaxed as he laid the table for breakfast with fresh papaya and plaited bread, thickly sliced.

He looked up as she appeared in the doorway, saw her face and immediately took out a chair. Thankfully she sat down, her hair still in damp, honey-coloured tendrils, the huge shirt completely covering the too-big shorts. He brought a fan-heater and switched it on near her chair, then still in the same easy silence placed a steaming cup of coffee in front of her.

She took the cup in both hands, intent on controlling the ridiculous shivering and then making a rapid exit. It was crazy; she'd spent two-and-a-half weeks in Hawaii without speaking more than a dozen words to any man, and yet here she was having breakfast with one, and a complete stranger at that.

The coffee was delicious, and he'd laced it strongly with rum. No doubt he thought she looked as if she needed it. Leila's immense brown eyes observed him warily over the rim of her cup. He was sitting across the table from her, dark hair still wet and untidy, his jaw blue-black with beard growth, the clear grey eyes watching her with an expression she couldn't fathom. Obviously he was waiting for an explanation. Half-heartedly she picked at her fruit, then put the spoon down. 'Mr Parnell?'

'Matt,' he interrupted. 'It's my name, please use it.'

She lowered her head in agreement. 'All right. Matt. I'm sorry to have been so hysterical on the beach. I lost someone by drowning about nine weeks ago and it seems I haven't got over it yet.'

The watchful eyes flickered and were steady again. 'I see. It was someone important to you?'

She hesitated, bracing herself for more questions. 'Yes.'

He was silent for a moment. Then he said, 'Wouldn't it be easier for you away from the sea?'

'Yes,' she agreed woodenly. 'Yes, it would be easier

away from the sea.' The implication that she had, in fact, chosen to be by the sea because it was *not* easy hung unspoken between them.

Then quite suddenly he smiled for the first time. Fascinated, she watched as the beautiful mouth formed the smile, revealing square white teeth. It transformed the tough, alert face into one of startling attractiveness. 'Are you feeling warmer now? Let me get you some more coffee.'

With those mundane phrases he dismissed her tragic revelation, her highly strung behaviour, and treated her as a pleasant companion sharing an early breakfast.

Leila smiled back at him and felt some of the tension ease from between her shoulder blades. She buttered a piece of bread with a pretence of hunger. 'Did you say you're on holiday here?'

'Yes, for two weeks. Some American friends offered me this house when I said I needed a holiday, far away from England and work. I get my own meals, soak up the sun, do a little wind-surfing.' Then he added casually, 'It's a complete change from the building trade back home.'

She raised her eyes quickly. 'Building? What particular line?'

That upward slant of the lips was there again. Clearly the devastating smile was not in frequent use. 'Housing as well as bigger stuff,' he said. 'My own firm. Medium sized, moderate capital. Don't let me start on business or I'll bore you to death.'

'My father was in building and developing,' Leila said quietly. 'I was always interested in everything that went on at the sites.'

Again that odd expression passed fleetingly across his face. He opened his mouth to say something, changed his mind, and then asked, 'So you did say "Garland"? Your father was George Garland of Garland Developments?'

'Yes,' agreed Leila gently. 'He died three months ago.'

'I know,' he said, and looking straight into her eyes, 'I'm sorry.'

'Thanks,' she said simply. 'And thanks for the breakfast. I'll go back to the hotel now, and let you have the clothes later.'

He said nothing to detain her, asked no more questions, made no further mention of her father. The tightness in her throat eased and she breathed more freely as she opened the door. 'I like the kitchen,' she said, looking round her belatedly.

'Well, this is Hawaii Five-O. The fiftieth state of America. Therefore the kitchens are good, and the plumbing excellent. That much at least America has done for Hawaii.' He indicated a bright yellow beach buggy parked by the back gate. 'Hop in. I'll take you back.'

With barely concealed relief Leila took the passenger seat. If she didn't get back to her room soon she'd fall asleep where she was. A few moments later early risers among the hotel guests were intrigued to see the Garland girl wearing a gaudy shirt twice too big for her dropped at the gate by a big unshaven guy. Knowingly they winked and nudged. Some exchanged a smile. 'These quiet ones,' they said, 'they're always the worst.'

Matt Parnell sat in the beach buggy and watched her thoughtfully as she walked away from him. When she reached the hotel entrance he saw her lift the heavy hair from her neck and flip it backwards; the first time he'd noticed her touch it. He smiled ruefully to himself and ran a hand raspingly over his jaw. No other woman of his acquaintance would have gone in and out of the water, then changed their clothes, then sat down to breakfast, without so much as touching their hair.

Her apparent lack of interest in her appearance certainly put him in his place. Without another glance at the hotel he set the bright little vehicle hurtling along the road inland.

CHAPTER TWO

IT was the next afternoon before Leila saw him again. Thirty-two hours later, and she'd spent twenty of those asleep. Six hours flat out when she got back early that morning, and then a long, long night of unbroken sleep after sunbathing on her balcony.

She didn't go in for self-analysis, but she could see quite clearly that her hysterical outburst on the beach had released more of the tension which gripped her. And those few words about her father and the building trade—what a chain of thought they had set off. With a lift of the heart she recognised that she'd taken one more step towards deciding what to do with her future.

She was conscious of gratitude to the man, Matt Parnell. He hadn't fussed, yet his very lack of comment had underlined his concern. Even more reassuringly, he hadn't attempted the smallest pass. An unusual man, and one who'd helped more than he knew. She almost looked forward to seeing him again when she returned the borrowed clothes.

It was hot, as usual, that afternoon, so she put on a cream silk dress with inserts of lace and slipped dark blue sandals on her bare feet. Leaving the hotel, she headed for the shady side of the road to wait for the tourist bus to Ala Moana Park and the shopping area there.

Matt Parnell uncoiled himself from his beach buggy at the edge of the pavement and stood blocking her path. 'Hello there. I've been waiting to see if you came out of the hotel. I want company on a helicopter trip to some of the little islands, and I thought I might persuade you to come with me.'

She looked up at him. In denim shorts and a fine cotton shirt he looked cool, comfortable and infinitely capable. 'To the little islands?'

'Yes. We could land where and when we like, eat

16

picnic food, and perhaps have a swim.' She could see that he watched her reaction to the mention of swimming, but she had herself well in hand and showed nothing.

'I was about to go shopping at Ala Moana, but I could go back and change, I suppose.'

He didn't pretend that it was an enthusiastic acceptance, or that a silk and lace dress would be ideal for island hopping by helicopter. He just shrugged easily. 'If you want to go I'll wait here while you change. I've got the food.'

Rather to her own surprise Leila went straight back to her room and put on a white bikini under blue shorts and a sun-top, wondering as she did so what he would have done for a companion if she hadn't showed up. She went down, tossed her canvas beach-bag behind the seat and stood there expectantly.

'Great,' he said. 'Let's go.'

They drove to the heliport, where he lifted their bags and the picnic basket out of the buggy and made for the office. 'Right,' he said, turning back to her with the formalities completed. 'It's the white one over there.'

She looked around, puzzled. 'But—are you the pilot?'

'Yes, Ma'am.' He spoke in an exaggerated American accent, and bestowed on her the rare and brilliant smile. 'All qualified and competent. I've hired the machine for the rest of the day.'

Then with no fuss at all they were airborne, banking and turning out to sea in a steep arc and leaving the high volcanic peaks of Oahu behind them. Leila had flown by helicopter before, and she liked it. 'Do you pilot planes as well?'

'Yes. I have a licence, although I don't fly very often. But I do keep a helicopter at home. It's useful for visiting the sites.'

She kept silent, while a small warning bell sounded insistently in her mind. She was getting involved with this man, heading out to sea with him as heedlessly as a teenager with her boyfriend instead of a woman of twenty-six who had no intention of letting any man dominate her life again. Not that Matt Parnell dominated, exactly. He was capable, he evidently liked his own way and knew how to get it, but underneath she was certain he was kind and she liked him. As long as she didn't like him too much ... Her thoughts were reflected in her eyes, careful and extremely wary.

'I flew one a few days ago,' he went on nonchalantly, 'and found a tiny island, hardly more than an atoll. It was peaceful and very lovely, so I decided to do it again. A boat would have been good, but we'd have had to find an island that was accessible through its reef. The helicopter is noisier, but much more convenient.'

Leila watched his hands on the controls. They were large and brown with square nails kept very clean, and dark hairs curled at the wrists and up the muscular forearms. A faint relief enveloped her—she'd never cared for hairy men. Hastily she gave herself a mental shake and sat up straighter, looking down as they sped away from Oahu.

The sea was blue-green, shot with glittering points of light from the sun. From such a height those enormous waves looked like a series of ripples, and she could see the famous black beaches whose orgins lay in long-past volcanic activity. Lying north-west was another mountainous island. 'That's Kanai,' said Matt, 'but we're giving it a wide berth and heading west to that little cluster on the horizon.'

In the distance she could see what appeared to be dark green rocks fringed with silver, but as they flew closer she saw that they were a group of small islands, each with its shallow lagoon inside a coral reef, surrounded by the rollers of the Pacific.

He circled slowly, losing height. 'Which do you fancy?'

There was something intensely fascinating about flying around and choosing which island appealed to her. She pointed, staring down intently. 'That one!'

He shot her a look, amused, then circled once more and landed accurately on firm white sand, with top-heavy palms and a belt of thick undergrowth behind them. 'There you are,' he said calmly. 'One uninhabited

island all to ourselves and every bit of a quarter of a
mile long.'

He took her hand as she jumped out, and Leila drew
in a deep breath. An unfamiliar sensation was taking
hold of her. She felt a bubbling excitement, a keen
interest in their surroundings; an urge to talk non-stop,
to chatter about anything. They walked along the
shining beach for a moment, and when she turned she
saw two sets of footprints following them along the
white sand. It was then that she identified the sensation
which gripped her. It seemed a long time since she'd
experienced it. She was enjoying herself.

Late that night Leila sat on her bed, watching a full
yellow moon as it hung theatrically over the palms. She
circled bent knees with her arms and went back over
each moment of her outing with Matt. She was
astounded at the way she had done and said things
which hitherto had been impossible.

The first incredible thing had been that she swam in
the lagoon and enjoyed it. True, she had already been
wearing her bikini, but not with any real intention of
entering the water. After a barefoot walk together,
chatting lazily about nothing in particular, Matt had
stripped to his trunks, held out a hand, and said,
'Coming?'

And the strange thing was, that feeling completely
safe, she had slipped out of her shorts and sun-top and
plunged into the water with him. Something she had
never thought she could face again after wading
through the shallows of the relentless surf as they
brought in Lance's body. Maybe at the back of her
mind had been a hazy picture of herself running
hysterically into the water back on Oahu, and then
being lifted up and deposited safely on dry land.

Whatever the reason, she had swum lazily in the
sheltered lagoon, cut off by the coral reef from the
ocean itself. It seemed strange to have Matt in the water
with her, swimming almost within touching distance.
Lance hadn't been like that. He'd been like quicksilver,
in and out of the waves, diving and weaving, bobbing

up in front of her, circling her waist and pulling her close for salty kisses. It was all so different with Matt, and she knew that one more chain binding her tensed-up inner self had been severed with awesome ease.

From time to time during that sunlit afternoon she glimpsed the man beneath the undemanding and considerate companion, but always the male-female relationship was relegated to unimportance, almost ignored. She knew perfectly well that men liked to see her in a bikini; it had been apparent since her teens, but never more than during her time on the world's beaches with Lance. She accepted the fact and then ignored it, pleased and yet half-irritated by the attention she attracted.

When they came out of the water Matt threw her a towel, and there, in those cool grey eyes, had been an acknowledgement of her attraction, her femininity. For a moment he became still as his glance took in her wet body with the scraps of white cotton clinging like a second skin. She tensed, ready to rebuff him, but there was no need. He made no move towards her, no comment, just turned away for the picnic basket. They sat beneath the palms and ate crusty Hawaiian bread with fresh crab-meat and salad, drank pineapple juice and champagne, spooned up passionfruit ice-cream out of small wood and metal freezers. It was the most appetising meal she'd eaten for months.

Afterwards, gratitude overcame her. She was lying on a towel, her hair spread to dry in the sun. 'Thanks, Matt,' she said simply. 'I was finding it impossible to go into the sea since—since nine weeks ago. You made it easy.'

'Where did it happen?' he asked quietly.

'Australia. Johanna Beach ... It was Lance, my boyfriend, who was drowned. He was a championship surfer. I'd been with him for about eight months.'

He nodded, his mouth lifting at one corner in the way that was becoming familiar. His chin was propped on his hands with his elbows sunk in the sand. 'If he was a top surfer why was he drowned?'

'It's a dangerous sport, even for experts. The weather

was foul and the surf enormous. We'd quarrelled and he went out in a rage. Not ideal conditions for safety.'

She stopped. It seemed unbelievable to have said as much as she had, after nine long weeks of complete silence. It was beyond her to say why they'd quarrelled, or to tell him of the bizarre funeral with only herself and a handful of surfing friends present. Silently she lay there, her memories accompanied by the distant crash of the breakers.

But Matt went on to speak of other things. 'Do you work for a living, Leila?'

'Not up to now,' she admitted. Here was another of her hang-ups being given an airing. 'I've qualified in landscape design, though. I took a post-grad. degree in that so as to work for my father. I always liked the practical side of building, especially planning the sites and seeing the grounds or gardens being laid out. When I left school I took Fine Arts, which I loved. But it wasn't really a training for anything specific in the building trade, and I spent a year getting under Dad's feet and everyone else's before going back to university for two years to study landscape design itself. I was all set to join him in the firm when I met Lance.'

Once again she dried up. At this rate he'd have her entire life history before they even got back in the helicopter. He might look tough but he must be pure putty to keep on listening to her.

'And what now?' he asked.

'I've decided to start work at last, although it's too late to work with Dad.' Hang-up number three, she thought wearily. 'But it's still a family firm. I'll try working for Garlands.'

It was said. The decision made. Suddenly she felt content. Though why she should detect consternation on Matt's face she had no idea. She would ask him, in a minute. But first she would just close her eyes. The sun was warm and she felt utterly at peace. Then without even the courtesy of asking him about his own affairs she fell fast asleep where she lay, the bikini drying on her golden body and the sun-streaked hair still spread above her head.

She was wakened by Matt's hand on her arm. 'Rise and shine. Time to go back. There's a squall blowing up. Nothing much, but we'd be better out of it.'

Wide-eyed and put out, she sat up. She felt at a disadvantage having been asleep while he sat there wide awake. The sun was low over the sea, the palms waved restlessly above, and Matt was back in his shirt and shorts, looking dark and impatient against the wide expanse of sky. She jumped to her feet and pulled on her shorts. 'How long have I been asleep?'

'Two hours or so,' he said calmly.

'But why didn't you waken me? You wanted company on your trip and I've hardly been that, have I, flat out on my towel?'

She couldn't fathom the look on his face. 'I'm not complaining,' he said.

The flight was quick, with clouds chasing them and a brief tropical shower obliterating the helicopter field as they landed. The air was heavy with the scent of wet flowers as he drove her back. It was embarrassing but she was yawning once more. 'Thanks again, Matt. It was lovely.'

'You'd better get some more sleep,' he advised with a slight smile. 'I'll be in touch.' The level grey gaze lingered on her face for a moment, and then he sped away along the coast road, leaving her staring blankly after him.

She had supper in her room and watched the moon come up. It was odd, but though tension and guilt still weighed on her spirit, she felt that at last she could admit to them, examine them. Impulsively she opened one of her cases and took out a photograph. Framed in leather, well-worn from constant packing and unpacking, it was a picture of a man in his late fifties, with blunt features, grizzled hair and intent brown eyes.

Leila gazed at it. 'Hello again, Dad,' she said quietly, and ran one finger round the frame in silent apology for keeping it at the bottom of a suitcase for three months. It wasn't unbearable any more to look at that well-loved face. All at once the tears came, the first she'd shed for him, and with something close to relief she let them flow unhindered.

Much later the maid came to clear away her supper things and she got ready for bed. But she didn't settle down for sleep. There was too much to think about, too much to decide. Every instinct was urging her to get away from Matt Parnell. He was too good to be with, too kind, too *attractive*, and she had no intention of getting even remotely involved with him or any other man. She sat on the bed, staring out into the night. Then she picked up the phone.

'Get me Honolulu Airport, please. Yes, I know it's late, but if possible I want a flight home tomorrow instead of in three days' time.'

She walked along the road to the headland, carrying the freshly laundered shorts and shirt. She had to return them, and could hardly just dash off without so much as a thank you. The sun was already high, she'd wakened late and there was just time to visit the beach-house before the hotel car took her to the airport.

The road sloped down towards the next beach, where the lagoon lay brassy and still under the sun. She could see the white beach-house with its tulip tree and the flare of scarlet blossoms, and the yellow beach-buggy parked at the back, then it was all lost to view as the road dipped and curved.

Moments later the sound of an engine warned her to step on to the sandy verge, and before she could gather her wits a beach-buggy hurtled past. It was Matt's. He was driving and at his side was a girl with coiled dark hair, wearing a cerise dress and huge sun glasses.

They had gone past in a moment, not noticing her as she stood beneath a bauhinia tree just off the road. She looked helplessly at the clothes she carried. He wouldn't be there; she didn't have to say goodbye. He had gone out somewhere with a woman, a pretty one, but—she could leave the things for him and perhaps a note—she carried her straw bag and in it were some picture postcards she'd bought in the hotel.

She put the bag containing the shirt and shorts on the porch by the door, then sat on the top step biting her pen and wondering what to write. If the girl in the car had been someone special to Matt then obviously she must keep the note cool and friendly. No sentimental farewells just because he'd been kind and helped her more than he would ever know, no becoming involved—that was what she wanted, wasn't it? She took out a card and wrote:

Am flying home today. Thanks for lending me the clothes and for all your help and kindness.

Leila G.

It wasn't until she was slipping the card into the mailbox that she saw the picture on it. A tiny, coral-fringed island, uninhabited and remote. She almost snatched it back and wrote another. But why? He would think she'd chosen that particular one in recognition of their helicopter trip.

From the steps she looked down towards the lagoon where holidaymakers splashed and shouted. This part of her life was finished. Soon it would be just a memory. And so would Matt Parnell—a pleasant one.

It was cool and wet at Heathrow; another world, another life from that of Hawaii. Everything seemed muted, subdued. Grey skies instead of dazzling blue; the concrete jungle of the massive airport instead of the white skyscrapers and tropical flowers of Honolulu. She knew a moment's sense of loss for the vibrant life and colour of the Islands, and then it was gone. She was back in England . . . It was springtime in England.

She made for the long-stay car park and shivered as the breeze caught her, damp and faintly scented. It was her third return to England since Lane's death; nine weeks of travel without once going back to Warwickshire, never stopping more than a night in any place until Hawaii. That trip had been worthwhile. She felt a different person from the taut, guilt-ridden creature who had boarded the plane three weeks earlier.

It was good to see the low shape of the Jaguar XJS waiting for her. Sleek and cream-coloured, it had been her father's gift to her when she gained her degree in landscape design. Like all his presents, it showed a deep knowledge of her tastes and personality. At first she'd been secretly reluctant to part with her ageing Spitfire, but she soon preferred the XJS. It was one of her many regrets that it should have been her father's gift which had taken her to the remote Cornish beach where she met Lance, filling in time as a lifeguard until he saved enough money to go abroad again. Two weeks after their meeting the new car had been left in the garage at home when she flew with him to Hawaii for the surfing.

Jet-lag was pressing down on her with its deadening lassitude. She pushed it aside, rubbed her aching forehead, and stacked her cases in the back of the car. Then she headed north to pick up the motorway, eager to reach the fresh green fields of her home county.

It was early afternoon when she reached the village. Everything was quiet, bathed in watery sunlight after a quick shower. She drove up the hill towards the house. Arlene would be surprised to see her back; she could imagine her squeaks of astonishment, the flutter of activity. Leila liked her bird-brained little stepmother, even though she had never thought her good enough for her father.

Ardenfields stood on rising ground beyond the village, its warm red brick seeming to welcome her back. Daffodils and narcissi starred the lawns and the banks of the stream which wound through the grounds and emerged by the gates. Leila slowed for the little bridge and then drove up to the house.

She used her own key to unlock the heavy front door, and the familiar smell of home enveloped her; furniture polish, flowers, and another smell, that of expensive cigars. She sniffed. Bernard! Of course, the brand new Mercedes outside would be his. He must have bought it since they last met at the funeral. As company secretary of Garlands and a bachelor he wasn't short of money.

'Arlene! Hello!' There was a bump and a muffled shriek. Then a door opened and closed somewhere. Leila stood at the bottom of the wide staircase, looking up, as a figure appeared on the landing. It was Arlene, doll-like and curvaceous as ever, wearing a pink négligé. But she didn't smile, didn't squeak with excitement, didn't run down with a kiss of welcome.

'Leila. What are you doing here?' She shut the bedroom door hastily behind her and leaned over the rail.

'I came back early from Hawaii. I didn't think it mattered about letting you know. Where is everybody? Where's Agnes, and Jade and Maisie? Where's Bernard? It's his cigars I can smell, isn't it?'

Arlene looked down at her with barely concealed irritation, and sighed audibly. Leila was concerned. 'Aren't you well, Arlene? Have I got you out of bed?'

'No.' The tone was suddenly casual. 'I've just been having a shower. Bernard's here for a day or two. He's somewhere around—in his room, perhaps. We're going out for the afternoon to Coventry.'

'Oh.' Leila felt oddly deflated. 'How are you, Arlene?'

'Fine.' The widow of three months certainly looked healthy, if a trifle uncomfortable. 'Jade and Maisie are away for the day and I've given Agnes the day off as well.'

Leila concealed her surprise. It was unheard of for her stepmother to be without staff in the house. She hesitated, dampened by the lack of welcome and puzzled in the face of Arlene's unease. 'I'll bring in my things,' she said, and went to unload the car.

By the time she'd finished carrying stuff upstairs both Bernard and Arlene were in the sitting room. 'Hello, Bernard.' Leila put up her cheek to be kissed. It was a ritual that she knew he liked. Bernard must always play the role of big strong male. Overplay it, perhaps, with the great medallion swinging on its chain against his chest, clearly visible because the casual shirt was unbuttoned almost to his waist. Bernard didn't change.

It was then, as the scent of St Laurent cologne drifted past her face, that she understood. Just for a moment she had thought that a hint of Arlene's perfume was there as well. Carefully she observed them as they made a belated fuss of her. Yes, there was an air of slightly guilty excitement about them both. Conspiracy was too strong a word, but there was something between them.

Bernard, expensive and expansive and aggressively male, was even more pleasant than usual. She could have smiled. It was a free country and if they wanted to make love in the afternoon when they thought they would be undisturbed then that was their business, not hers. But ... she watched Arlene narrowly. Had this been going on while Dad was alive?

'And you're feeling a little better now?' Bernard was asking, concern in his voice.

Leila found she couldn't meet his eyes, so she watched intently as Arlene poured tea into the delicate china cups. 'Yes. I'm much better. As a matter of fact I'm glad you're here together so that I can tell you both at once. I'm hoping to join the firm at last. I want to come in on the landscaping side.' She smiled a trifle grimly. 'I want to start work.'

'But—you can't!' gasped Arlene, her round blue eyes swivelling in Bernard's direction. 'We've sold the firm, or at least agreed to a takeover. The deal went through a few days ago. We were going to tell you as soon as we heard where you were going after Hawaii. We thought you'd be pleased!'

Leila sat very still. 'Bernard?'

'It's true. As chief executor and trustee of your father's estate I was legally entitled to follow Arlene's instructions. I was in favour. She wanted to convert her shares to cash . . .' He fell silent.

'You've sold Garlands? Dad's firm. Without telling me?' It couldn't be true. They were joking. But a glance at Bernard's heavy face, uncomfortable, but with a certain smugness about it, and Arlene's, pretty as a fairy doll with the red lips pressed obstinately together, showed her that this was no joke.

'How were we supposed to know you'd care?' asked Arlene tightly. 'You've hardly shown your face here since you fell for that—that boy. Your money has been taken care of for years, hasn't it? You had cash, but mine was tied up in the firm. So I decided to take it out. To sell up. And Bernard agreed with me.'

'I'm sure he did.' Leila rose from her chair. 'May I ask who has bought the firm?'

'Parnell Enterprises,' said Bernard. 'They're a very——'

But Leila didn't wait to hear more. She was making for the stairs, the sitting-room door closed quietly behind her.

CHAPTER THREE

ARLENE and Bernard left the house soon after their announcement, and in the silent hours that followed it had taken all Leila's will-power to stop herself sliding back into self-doubt. Honesty made her admit that since meeting Lance she'd taken little interest in the firm. Bernard could hardly be blamed for not consulting her, and of course he was right in saying that he had the authority to negotiate a takeover bid for Garlands.

Her own income was not dependent on the firm, she owned no shares in it; but Arlene's part of the Garland estate was the house and land, funds for their upkeep, and the income from a majority holding in the company. An adequate bequest, some might say a very generous one, but not enough for Arelne, apparently. She had always been openly and rather engagingly mercenary, an aspect of her personality which was at odds with the pretty little bird-brain image she projected. Leila thought it had been naive to imagine that her stepmother would be satisfied with a luxurious home and a steady income.

The staff returned at six o'clock, and finding Leila back made a fuss of her; Jack putting away the XJS so tenderly she almost expected him to kiss it good night, while his wife Maisie bustled about preparing supper. As for Agnes, housekeeper since Leila's childhood, she clumped around forbiddingly, issuing a disjointed commentary in her dated jargon. 'Not at all considerate . . . They could at least have dined at home on your first night back . . . What was the mistress thinking of? . . . And you flying halfway around the world, Miss Leila, and looking like a ghost, for all you say you feel fine . . .'

Leila was comforted by their concern for her. She went to bed very early, reflecting bleakly that the only

29

genuine words of welcome had come from the servants.
Much later, she awoke to hear Arlene and Bernard
come back. He went off noisily to one of the guest
rooms and Arlene to the big room she'd shared with
Leila's father. So they were keeping up a front of mere
friendship and shared business interests when they
weren't alone in the house.

Her mind went back to Matt Parnell not telling her
about his takeover of Garlands ... The knife-sharp
thrust of dismay she'd felt when she heard that had
faded. Given time, she thought sleepily, he'd have told
me about it. I didn't give him the opportunity, that's
all. I left Hawaii in a hurry. She turned over and
thumped her pillow. She had no intention of re-
examining her reasons for that very speedy departure.

It was daybreak when she wakened, sweating and
trembling from the dream. There had been a sail-board
skimming silently across a lagoon, and as she watched
an immense breaker crashed over the reef and tossed
the red-sailed board like driftwood on the beach. But it
was Lance's body floating face downwards in the water
as, thigh deep, she struggled to drag him ashore.

The wind whistled and shrieked along the beach and
the surf swept forward greedily in immense glassy
curves. At last, sobbing and gasping, she dragged him
clear and turned him over. The lean golden back
became a dark hairy chest, a flat stomach, powerful
thighs and brawny arms. Black hair lay wet against the
forehead and the jaw was dark with beard-growth. The
eyes were open, but they weren't Matt's clear and grey,
they were Lance's. Blue, vivid blue, gazing sightlessly
up at the pink-tinged sky.

The house was silent except for the rasp of her
breathing. She felt weak with relief at the sight of her
familiar bedroom in the faint light of dawn. Exhausted,
she lay back against the pillows and wiped the tears
from her cheeks.

Breakfast was unpleasant. Arlene, beautifully made-
up as always, but a trifle heavy-eyed, had come to table
instead of being served in her room. She adopted a
matter-of-fact attitude about the takeover, while

Bernard presented Leila with a detailed statement of the winding up of the firm, along with smoothly worded advice to 'go and see the legal chaps' about her own financial position ... 'Even though you weren't a shareholder your father stipulated a sum to be paid to you should dissolution or takeover of the company take place. This will be done, of course, according to his instructions ...'

'What about you and Arlene? You were both principal shareholders. Does your cut come as ready cash?'

'Well, of course it does,' said Arlene. 'That's the object of it all. I want to know exactly what I'm worth. I want cash—Bernard understands that. Stocks and shares float up and down and keep the capital tied up.'

'All right,' said Leila, 'so you're going to get what you want. Might I ask what's happening to the men?'

Arlene shrugged. 'Building workers are being laid off all over the country. Those employed at the moment have a job as long as their particular scheme is going. After that it's up to Parnells.'

Bernard nodded in agreement, intent on his kedgeree, while Leila eyed her own small helping with something like revulsion. Then Arlene spoke again. 'Another thing, Leila. About the house——' She slapped Bernard's restraining hand from her arm. 'No, Bern, she's got to know. The house is being put up for sale very soon.' Her baby-blue eyes had taken on the pebble-like quality which meant that she was not to be swayed. 'There's no rush, but if you could look round for somewhere to stay when you're in this country ... I'm buying a little place in Belgravia for myself. You know I've always wanted to get back to London.'

Leila stared at her while one thought spun round and round in her mind. She doesn't like me. Arlene *doesn't like me*. Why hadn't she realised it before? Her stepmother had always been pleasant enough with her, almost affectionate at times. But—Leila felt the familiar chill of tension between her shoulder blades—that had all been while Dad was alive. Just now she had said, 'Look round for somewhere to stay', when she knew that Ardenfields was Leila's home. Bernard was embarrassed, and so became pompous. 'Did you hear Arlene, my dear?'

'Yes. I heard. You're putting the house up for sale.' *Arlene didn't like her.* With an effort Leila kept her voice from trembling. 'What about Agnes and Jack and Maisie?'

'That was in the will with all the other hand-outs,' Arlene said lightly. 'Surely you remember? If the house is sold before they retire it's lump sums all round and glowing references. If they retire from here it's lump sums again. How can they lose? In any case, I think anyone with the money to buy this place will be glad to take on reliable staff.'

Leila relaxed a little. Her father had known loyalty from his servants, and had taken steps to see that it was rewarded. She searched her memory for the long and tortuous wording of his will; the countless provisos, the added clauses. At the time of its reading she had been so stunned by his death, so remorseful, that she hadn't taken it in, much to Lance's fury when he questioned her back in Australia.

She swallowed. Her mouth tasted dry and stale and she reached for more orange juice instead of her coffee. A picture came to her of her father's well-loved figure hunched over his desk, working out the best way to care for his dependants; while his daughter roamed the world's beaches with a handsome money-grabber and his wife flexed greedy fingers in the background. Oh Dad—

Suddenly she felt the urge to leave the house. 'I'll find a place of my own,' she said flatly, 'and I'll be out within the month.'

Leaving them both protesting that there was no need for such haste she went up to her own domain; sitting-room, bedroom and bathroom at the back of the house, overlooking the orchard and the peaceful fields beyond. The rooms had been her refuge since her father built the house when she was ten years old. She halted at the door, one hand upraised against the frame. She was cutting loose from the old way of life and now it looked as if she would have no choice but to cut loose from the old home as well.

She went to the window and stared out at the damp countryside, puzzling as to why her father had made no ruling about the house staying in the family when he had known how she loved it. He couldn't have hoped she would marry Lance and live elsewhere, so should she take it as his way of saying she must get out and do something with her life?

There was still her own inheritance to check up on. Strange that she felt not the slightest inclination to do so. She smiled grimly. Years of mixing with students from all walks of life had taught her some inescapable truths about the 'haves' and 'have-nots'. She would have felt plenty of inclination to check on her finances if she'd been down to her last ten pounds instead of the sum in her bank account.

Bleakly she stood there, gripping the oak window-ledge. Whatever happened she was not going back to a life of moneyed leisure; she'd tried that with Lance and it had been a disaster. Generations of Garlands had bequeathed to her a passion for hard work and achievement. Blacksmiths, thatchers, carpenters, stone-masons and finally builders had passed on a heritage of creative ability backed by sound business sense.

She thought of the little girl whose school holidays had been spent trailing around building sites with her father; the teenager who had replanned the grounds of Ardenfields with more enthusiasm than expertise; the Fine Arts student receiving her First with a moist-eyed father frantically applauding . . .

She would do as she had decided back in Hawaii. Go into landscape work. Garlands was gone; there would be no position in the family firm. But there were other jobs, other opportunities. She'd do it the same way as anyone else—on her merits.

The pile of architects' journals were in the cupboard where Agnes had stacked them month by month. She took the top three and began to go through them, lips jutting obstinately in a way her father would have recognised.

It was worse than she'd expected. Few jobs were advertised, and they demanded experience both in design and in practical work. Two were for posts with local authorities, one with a private firm of architects, and one for an assistant to a landscape gardener. Nothing that was suitable for a recently qualified landscape designer.

After ten minutes she sat back, having gone through the quarterly *Landscape Design* and all the issues of *Architects' Journal*. She wouldn't stand a chance without practical experience—and yet her years on and around building sites had given her just that—but not in the way that counted, not in actual employment.

She'd known things were difficult, of course. From time to time she'd heard from Dee Williams, her special friend at university, who'd told her how the others were getting on. Five of the men had landed jobs in landscape design and two of the women. Of the others, two men were still unemployed and the other two women were employed as a waitress and a mother's help.

Leila sat at her desk and faced the fact that she might not get a job. And if she did, it was unlikely to be the sort of work she really wanted—large-site work. She loved gardens and all growing things but she couldn't see herself planning a colourful roof garden in Chelsea, or deciding on potted plants for a patio in Solihull. The very real challenge of small-scale designing left her unmoved.

And there was another aspect which disturbed her; that of whether she was right in even *trying* for a job in the present economic climate ... She didn't need the money, and if she didn't get work she wouldn't have to stand in the dole queue.

She thought of the Garland construction sites; the superb small developments of private housing, the various projects dear to her father's heart such as sheltered accommodation for the elderly, and knew there would have been worthwhile work for her with the firm.

But—the thought leapt forward aggressively from the

back of her mind—she knew Matt Parnell. He had
seemed kind, even concerned, and he had taken over
her father's firm. Could she ask him . . .?

For a few moments she considered the idea of
approaching him and asking for a job. For a few
moments, that was all. She was an independent woman
and wanted no favours; she couldn't trade on her close
connection with Garlands just because she happened to
know the new owner of the firm.

She thought of their helicopter trip to that tiny, coral-
fringed island; of two sets of footprints studding the
firm white sand; of the big, confident man who had
helped her to sort out her own chaotic emotional state.
It might seem that he had done little—had merely
enjoyed an outing with a pretty girl, but Leila knew that
the time spent in his carefully undemanding company
had helped her more than anything else.

And that was enough. No more help from Matt
Parnell. She reached for the *Architects' Journals* for a
final look. The words 'The Cowper Bequest' registered
with her only because she'd seen them in several copies.
Half-page adverts quite separate from the 'situations
vacant' section. 'The Cowper Bequest'—it sounded like
the title of an outdated thriller.

Only half-interested, she read on. The late Howard B.
Cowper had bequeathed both land and money for the
building of a major sports complex and leisure centre in
the West Midlands. Contracts had been placed with the
architects and builders but now, in accordance with
Cowper's wishes, an open competition was being held
for the landscaping of the site.

A tightness in her chest and the thud of her heart
made Leila aware that for several seconds she had
stared at the printed page without breathing. Could this
possibly be the opportunity she was looking for?
Midlands-born or Midlands-based landscape designers
were invited to submit high-quality schemes, and to put
in preliminary applications to the Cowper Foundation's
rooms in Birmingham, where details of the site and
copies of the building plans would be available to
entrants.

Leila felt rather as if her eyes were about to pop straight out of her head. It was so much on her wavelength it was unbelievable. So where was the snag? There must *be* one. Ah!—'positively the last date for preliminary applications—April 23rd.' Tomorrow! And 'last date for submission of entries—May 21st.' Only four weeks hence!

She scattered the pile of journals, searching for back numbers. The announcement had first appeared six months earlier. She bit her lip. It was nobody's fault but her own that she hadn't seen it earlier; and if she'd kept in closer touch with Dee or some of the others she would doubtless have heard about it from them. They were probably all working like maniacs on it at this very moment.

She opened a cupboard and took out a huge roll of plans—the major design she'd worked on for her degree. Eight enormous sheets containing detailed lay-outs for playing fields, tennis courts, an open-air swimming pool and a huge indoor sports and leisure centre. Every tree, every shrub, every flower annotated and listed, along with the make-up of paths, terraces, car parks, details of land-drainage, culverts, storm drains, and future maintenance.

When placed side by side the eight sheets almost covered the floor of her sitting-room. The design had been the most difficult and gruelling task of her life, but it had confirmed her degree in Landscape Design and earned her the prize for the best design of her year. Even now she felt a twinge of surprised pride when she looked at it.

It didn't mean, however, that she could sail in and win the Cowper competition. But it did mean she wasn't out of the running if she could incorporate some of her ideas from the degree designs into an entry. One thing was certain—she would never have the time to start from scratch. Now if the soil on the site should be similar to that on which she'd based her selection of plants ... and if the total land area for the Cowper scheme wasn't too much different ...

But first—she must get the preliminary form and fill

it in. With a speed and energy which had long been
absent from her movements she rushed into her
bedroom to change. Her hair, newly washed, swung
almost to her shoulders in heavy sun-streaked waves.
She made up her eyes, left her golden skin untouched
and brushed her lips with colour. Then she put on a
cream silk shirt and a suit in caramel-coloured worsted.

Picking up her camera and some spare film she went
downstairs to find her indispensable wellies and some
plastic bags for soil samples. Five minutes later she
zoomed off in the XJS, leaving Jack smiling fondly,
Agnes mystified at her speedy departure, and Bernard,
who thought she was going to search for a flat, highly
uncomfortable.

The traffic was heavy as she drove into the centre of
Birmingham but, as always, she was conscious of her
affection for the great sprawling mass of the city;
reflecting ruefully that she rarely, if ever, heard a good
word said about it. True, there was heavy industry
concentrated over a massive area, there was high-rise
housing that was probably the despair of local
authorities where once it had been the pride; and there
was old property cheek by jowl with brash new
developments. But it was England's second city and
with all its faults, she loved it.

She had to keep her wits about her because, as usual,
a variety of male drivers had their eyes on the car. A
luxury sports car with a sun-tanned blonde at the wheel
seemed to bring out the worst in some of them. They
tried tooting and all the tricks known as 'carving up',
ostensibly having fun but in reality displaying more
than a touch of aggression. She sighed in resignation as
she went up and down through the gears. So much for
sex equality when it came to being behind a wheel.

The Cowper rooms were in a solid Victorian building
just off Temple Row. Appropriate, she thought, to have
the trustees of a millionaire housed in the city's banking
quarter. An elderly clerk, polite and efficient, gave her a
huge roll of plans and a form to fill in.

A clock ticked loudly, creating an illusion of isolation
and tranquillity even though the busy thoroughfare was

only yards away. Pen poised, Leila hesitated at the first item: *Name* ... In an instant she resolved that nobody should know she was entering; not Bernard or Arlene, not any of the ex-Garland men, not even any of her former colleagues on the course. She left that and filled in her qualifications.

The door crashed open and a dark-suited young fellow with tightly curled hair dashed in. 'Hi! Sorry I'm late. Where are the others?'

The elderly clerk smiled gravely, coughed, looked meaningly at Leila and said quietly, 'In the board room, *waiting*, Mr Robin.'

'Mr Robin' swung round to look at Leila. His dark eyes liked what they saw, and showed it. In return, and almost without realising it, her clear brown gaze took on the glacial quality which had warned off so many men. For a few seconds longer he stared, then shrugged. 'Good morning,' he murmured finally, and hurried away.

She dismissed him from her mind and returned to the form, trying to think of a pseudonym. She could hardly use John Smith, so she printed the first name that came to her—J.T. Rose. Why J.T. she had no idea. And Rose—well—because she liked roses. She liked delphiniums and nasturtiums, come to that, and dozens of other flowers, but they'd hardly do for a surname. As for her address; she hesitated again, and finally wrote: 'In process of moving—not yet settled.'

Then she handed the form to the clerk, checked the locality of the site, and made for the car park. The sense of dynamism and bustling energy that was Birmingham came to her and brought with it a surge of confidence. There was a freshness in the air, with a fitful sun bestowing the luminous April brilliance unique to an English spring. It didn't occur to her to go for a coffee or to look at the shops. The very act of doing something constructive towards her future had wiped everything else from her mind.

The site was well outside the city itself, so keeping the map beside her she drove towards the exit of the car park, and was almost out in the traffic when she noticed a muddy Range Rover slowing down for the entrance a short distance up the road. A big, dark-haired man was at the wheel, and acting purely on instinct Leila braked and slewed round in her seat to get a better view of him. Surely it was Matt Parnell?

Horns tooted angrily behind her and the Range Rover moved out of sight. She had no option but to go forward, trying to concentrate on the road but with half her mind on the man. Was she mad? Imagining she'd seen someone in the heart of Birmingham who was actually in Hawaii, and all because she'd had a ghastly dream about him and had considered asking him for a job?

At the next turning she was off, almost without thought, zooming round a left-hand bend that would take her back to the car park. She didn't begin to feel foolish until she was circling the ranks of parked cars searching for the high bulky shape of the Range Rover.

It wasn't there. Whoever it was had gone, perhaps unable to find a place. With a ridiculous sense of let-down she edged out into the traffic again and headed away from the city centre. Obviously that impulsive streak of hers hadn't yet been conquered.

She drove on through a leafy suburb, the factories left behind, until at last she saw the motorway ahead and knew she was getting nearer. Stopping, she studied the map, then turned down a bumpy road and along a dirt track bordering waste land. A group of builders' huts were there, locked and deserted, but a small neat notice said 'The Howard B. Cowper Foundation'.

She got out and looked round. No building work begun as yet, thank goodness. A rubbish-dump flanked a group of playing fields while the motorway snaked overhead and beyond them. There was a stretch of stagnant water and at the other end of the site a high railway embankment.

Quickly she slipped out of the flimsy suede shoes and put on her wellies. Far from being dismayed at the unpromising site, she was encouraged. The land she'd been allocated for her degree designs had been far worse but she'd enjoyed the challenge of transforming it, if only on paper.

She slung the camera round her neck and grabbed her sketch-book and pencils, then with the heavy wellies beneath her elegant suit she clumped eagerly across the rough ground.

It was late afternoon by the time she drove up the hill to Ardenfields. She'd spent ages at the Cowper site sketching, taking photographs and digging for earth samples, and now she felt ready for a long soak in the bath.

The huge 'For Sale' board at the gates took her unawares, giving her the mental equivalent of a punch in the ribs. Arlene wasn't losing any time! Leila pulled in at the side of the lane and stared thoughtfully at the house. Her father had built his home well. The dull pink brick looked as weathered and subdued as if it had been there a hundred years instead of a mere sixteen. It was a big house, well-proportioned and graceful, with established clematis and climbing roses making their new growth and softening its lines. Daffodils nodded on the great curving lawns, and the first faint green hazed the willows bordering the stream.

Tears pricked her eyelids even while common sense reminded her that she'd stayed away from home for months on end and had hardly given the place a thought. But she'd known it was *there*. There to come back to . . .

She went up the drive and received another surprise. A muddy Range Rover was parked near the front of the house—surely it was the one she'd seen in Birmingham?

Agnes opened the door as she reached it. 'There's a Mr Parnell waiting in the sitting-room, Miss Leila. He's been here nearly an hour and I've given him tea.'

Leila stopped dead and stared at her. 'Oh, thanks Agnes. Will you bring in some more for me?' With an odd reluctance she opened the sitting-room door. Matt was standing by the windows, dressed for the building site rather than for afternoon tea. He looked every bit as tough fully clothed as when he wore only swimming trunks back in Hawaii.

'Hello, Matt,' she said quietly. 'It *was* you, then, in Birmingham?'

His gaze took in her slim form in the expensive suit, and she wondered if he in turn was thinking of how he'd last seen her in a tiny bikini. The beautiful mouth lifted at one corner in the way she remembered, but he looked puzzled as he said, 'You saw me?'

'Yes, as I was leaving the car park, but I—judged I was mistaken in thinking it was you.' She felt awkward. More than that—she felt utterly crazy when she recalled how she'd zoomed around searching for him.

He watched her consideringly. 'I *did* see a blonde in an XJS,' he admitted, 'and I did think it looked like you. So as I was visiting a site not far from here I decided to pay a courtesy call.'

She looked up into his eyes, ridiculously relieved to see them clear, confident and grey; not vividly blue like the eyes of the dead man in her nightmare. 'But I didn't think you were due back yet from Hawaii.'

'No,' he agreed, 'I wasn't. But then, neither were you, as I recall,' He waited. Was he expecting an explanation for her early return? If so, he was due for a disappointment. 'Something cropped up in the business,' he continued, 'so I took the night plane to the States, and flew back from there.'

'You—you got my note, and the clothes?'

'Yes, thanks.'

'I'd hoped to say goodbye in person but you passed me in the beach-buggy, going away from the house.' She was annoyed to hear herself sounding apologetic. He was the one who had some explaining to do, surely? *He* had taken over Garlands.

When Agnes arrived with fresh tea and cakes, Leila was amused to see her bestow on Matt that rare curve of the lips which, with her, passed for a smile. So he'd found favour already? Not easy when dealing with Agnes. She watched as the housekeeper marched out, feeling oddly reluctant to continue the conversation. She took off her jacket and moved to a settee. 'Come and sit down, Matt. Would you like more tea?'

He sat opposite her and she saw how the china teacup looked ludicrously dainty in his grasp. Quite at ease, he sat there as if taking afternoon tea was an accepted aspect of the building trade.

Then he said, 'The real reason I've come in person instead of just phoning is that I wanted to apologise for not telling you about the takeover.' He neither looked nor sounded apologetic but she found herself believing he meant it. 'I would have done so, of course, but you left sooner than I expected.'

She nodded. 'That's why you seemed concerned that afternoon on the little island—when I told you I was going into the firm.'

'Yes. Until that moment I had no idea that you had anything of the kind in view and I realised you couldn't know about the takeover. I gather you've been told about it by now?'

'Oh, yes.' It was almost impossible not to sound bitter. She could even feel the familiar tightness around her mouth from clamping her lips too firmly together. 'I knew within ten minutes of arriving back.' Her thick silky lashes lifted, revealing eyes shadowed with regret as she looked round the big beautiful room. 'The house is up for sale as well, as I expect you noticed when you arrived.'

'I noticed,' he agreed. 'I'm sorry, Leila, if it's not what you wanted.'

The note of real sympathy was almost too much for her. She could handle almost any situation without tears, but genuine concern penetrated her defences. She swallowed and looked intently at her cup. 'I'm going to move into a flat,' she said brightly. 'I know just the sort of place I'd like.'

He stared at her thoughtfully. 'Leila, about a job. Perhaps I could help there?'

She kept focusing on the teacup. It was white and gold with a circlet of ivy leaves round the handle. There was a tight, trapped feeling inside her chest. No, she thought, no. No more involvement here. I'm not ready for it. I can't cope with it. 'Thanks, Matt,' she said aloud, 'but I want to sort myself out a bit first. I'm still re-thinking my future.' She hesitated, filled with guilt at not telling him about the Cowper competition, and said the first evasive thing that came into her head. 'I might go to Italy for a few weeks, or the South of France . . . I really don't know yet *what* I want to do.'

If he didn't believe her he gave no sign of it. The tough lean face betrayed no emotion, the steady eyes gazed thoughtfully into hers. 'If you do decide you need a job, I'll do what I can. Give me a ring and I'll see what's going. I often hear of tenants in some of my bigger houses who need advice on their gardens.'

So—like all the men, he imagined that women landscape designers handled only domestic stuff. The knowledge of her intentions regarding Cowper formed a mental wall between them, which he seemed to sense. 'I'll do what I can,' he repeated and stood up. 'My home number's in the Coventry book if you should need it.' He hesitated, then said abruptly, 'Leila, how are you feeling? I don't want to pry but you were a bit low in Hawaii and things can't have been easy since you got back . . .'

'I'm sorting myself out,' she said truthfully, thinking of her newfound ·dynamism that morning. 'I'll be all right, Matt, and thanks.' Then because he was kind, because he'd taken the trouble to find her and tell her himself about the takeover, she bestowed on him her truly beautiful smile. She was out of practice, it was true, but when she managed it the effect was something to see.

For several seconds he looked at her, then with a slight nod he moved to the door. 'If you're sure of that I'll leave you,' he said. 'I have to go over to Warwick now.'

But Leila had one or two things to ask him before he left. 'Just a minute, Matt. I'd like to know what's happening to the Garland work-force. Are they still in employment?'

Eyes narrowed, he stood there with one hand grasping the door knob. 'Yes.'

'And will you be able to keep them employed?'

'I hope so.'

'But you can't guarantee it?'

'I can guarantee that the developments they're working on at present will all be completed. I can guarantee that whatever jobs are contracted out to Parnells the ex-Garland workforce,' he emphasised the *ex*, 'will be treated exactly the same as the established Parnell men.'

'You've kept them all on, then?'

'Yes,' he said shortly. 'And they stand a better chance of regular work now than they did six weeks ago.'

She was unconvinced, but acutely conscious that only weeks ago she had travelled within a hundred miles of Garlands without so much as a thought for the firm's employees. 'All the takeovers I've come across have benefited the taker rather than the taken. How do I know this one isn't the same?'

'You don't. So you'll just have to take my word for it, won't you?'

'Bernard Grover gave me details of the transaction but it meant little to me. It was all high finance and accountancy. I'm more interested in the human aspect.'

'Very praiseworthy,' he commented drily.

Leila felt the colour mount in her cheeks. He was making her seem an interfering prig. She pushed at the sleeves of her shirt in an unconscious gesture of aggression. The heavy gold cuff-links withstood the strain and refused to budge. 'It's my father's firm and I think I'm entitled to ask.'

'It *was* your father's firm,' he corrected wearily. 'It's my firm now. Look—in a nutshell—three months ago I found myself stretched; for trained men, for equipment, the lot, but financially I was sound. In spite of the recession work kept coming in. I heard that Garlands were putting out feelers in the hope of a takeover. I went into it and saw it would be a good move, both for them and for me. I've come back from my first holiday in three years ready to work myself into the ground making sure it *is* a good move. And I don't expect to take so much as a weekend off, let alone visit Italy or the South of France——'

The grey eyes were cold as the sea in winter. 'I have

no ulterior motives,' he went on. 'I'm not a profiteer, and I have no intention of sending droves of chaps to join the dole queue. Is that quite clear?'

'Yes,' she said quietly. 'That's clear.'

'Then I'll be off.' Without more ado he left the room. A moment later the front door slammed behind him, and Leila was left standing by the tea-tray feeling foolish, resentful and uneasy.

CHAPTER FOUR

'ALL work and no play . . .' Agnes put the tray down with a thud.

'I know,' murmured Leila absently, 'it makes Jill a dull girl.' She laid aside her set-square and bit into a slice of Maisie's fruit cake. 'Honestly, Agnes, a few weeks' hard slog on my designs won't hurt me.'

Agnes eyed her critically. 'You look peaky to me,' she declared flatly. 'You don't go out, you don't see your friends. Even that nice Mr Parnell hasn't been round again——'

Leila sighed. Agnes was an incurable matchmaker, but only when she considered the man in question to be worth matching—or catching. Lance, on his one ill-starred visit to Ardenfields, had merited only a frigid greeting and after that a sniff or two, even though Leila had relegated him to a guest room for the duration of their visit. Matt, however, seemed to have made a hit.

'Look, Agnes, I hardly know Matt Parnell. Perhaps I'll meet him again sometime. It's possible.' But not likely. After that last encounter he wouldn't be in a hurry to seek her out. Since then she'd made it her business to check on the ex-Garland workforce, and found that what he'd said was true. As far as she could tell they were all fully employed and presumably happy in their work.

She turned back to her drawing board. 'I've got to finish this design, and until then I shall only leave the house to go and look at whatever flats the agents come up with.'

Agnes didn't answer. She'd been badly shaken by the news that the house was to be sold, and when Leila set out to inspect the first lot of flats she glimpsed tears behind the housekeeper's glasses. Like Jack and Maisie, Agnes had agreed to stay on if the new owner wanted her, but she was far from happy about it.

46

Leila knew how she felt, but could hardly see her own future lifestyle holding any place for a prim and elderly housekeeper. Agnes would be far happier staying at Ardenfields.

'Maisie wants to know what you'd like for lunch,' she said now.

'Oh, anything. Whatever my stepmother's having.'

'Mixed salad with low-calorie dressing, crispbread and black coffee.' Agnes didn't trouble to hide her disapproval.

'I'll have the salad but with a slice of Brie and some of Maisie's lemon mayonnaise. And a few wholemeal rolls—with butter.'

'That's more like it.' Agnes marched off, mollified, leaving Leila at the big drawing board by the window. There were only two weeks left before Cowper's closing date.

It had been a relief to find that she could use some of her degree designs without much alteration. Only some of them, though. The lake area had to be dealt with from scratch and the harsh line of the railway embankment needed careful treatment to soften it. She'd decided to only partly conceal the motorway fly-over, because she thought it a dramatic and graceful construction and wanted to let it enhance her design rather than attempt to block it from view completely.

Already the drawings showed the bold, imaginative sweep that was her especial talent, although such a style being so singularly suited to the Cowper development was sheer good luck. She was convinced that the site wanted nothing merely pretty; none of what she termed the itsy-bitsy stuff. Her ideas came not only from the proposed buildings but from the shape of the earth. If a site was flat and uninteresting then she changed it with a curve here, a rise there, a sharp fall or a gentle decline. Earth-shaping is the basis of all good landscaping. That was one of the things she hadn't needed to be taught. It seemed to her that she'd always known it.

Her plans for the areas to be wooded were down on paper. There were few established trees; hawthorns and sycamores around the tatty old playing fields, a few large willows bordering the water and, unexpectedly, three magnificent oaks at one end of the rubbish tip. The planting of semi-mature trees would be expensive, but money was not a crucial factor with the Cowper Foundation. She blessed Howard B. from the bottom of her heart. If the design had been aimed at a struggling local authority it would have had to be tackled very differently. She studied the architect's plans, pondering which combination of trees would complement the stark but imaginative buildings.

The house agent drove Leila across the Hagley Road towards Harborne. 'There's just one left,' he said dolefully. 'The last on our books. Top floor and attics, and rather pricey.'

Leila was pleasantly surprised when she saw the house. It was solid, spacious, and mercifully free from ornamentation. Not only that, the gardens showed signs of imaginative alteration and the road itself was secluded, with leaf-buds spattering its tree-lined length.

As for the flat ... It was a superb conversion, almost too good to be true; with an enormous open-plan living room and kitchen, and a bathroom and two bedrooms on a gallery floor which was reached by a spiral staircase. The main bedroom had a huge dormer window, and the bathroom boasted an original claw-foot bath with roses painted on the outside.

The fat Victorian flowers, overblown and deep pink, seemed to Leila to be a happy omen. J. T. Rose ... 'I'll take it,' she told the agent, and for the first time he smiled. So did Leila. She thought she could be happy in the flat, with its distinctive layout and solid, unpainted woodwork. She would be able to work in peace; there was room for the furniture that Arlene, surprisingly, had offered her from Ardenfields, and she would have an address to put on her Cowper entry which would reveal no connection whatsoever with the name of Garland.

Three days later she moved in. Agnes, Maisie and Jack had worked like mad, realising that this might be the last thing they could do for her. The furniture was all in place, a variety of pieces which Leila had loved for years and which her keen eye had seen as being well-suited to the flat. The spare bedroom was crammed with more items; and rugs, linen and kitchen equipment were all there ready for use without her having to spend precious time searching the shops for them.

It was Friday afternoon. Arlene was in London and the three servants were about to leave, so as to be back in time for her return. Agnes was putting on her coat and the inevitable felt hat, and looked suspiciously tight-lipped and flushed.

Half-expecting a sad farewell Leila went to the fridge and took out the bottle of champagne she'd bought specially for that moment. The cork popped. 'To all our futures,' she said gaily. The awkward moment passed and soon afterwards she waved from the window as they drove away.

She continued to stand there, vaguely surprised to feel only relief at being on her own instead of the wrenching sense of loss she'd expected. Down below a white Mini turned into the drive of the house next door and she watched with interest as two long elegant legs came into view. Leila hadn't met any of her neighbours in the house, much less those next door, so she waited and saw that the legs belonged to a slender body. Then she glimpsed a head of incredibly shiny brown hair, and leaned forward in astonishment. It surely wasn't Dee? Dee Williams, her friend from university? How had she known where to find her?

With a spurt of pure joy in her heart she made for the door and ran outside. Dee had gone into the wrong house, so Leila followed without ringing any bells and called, 'Dee. Where are you? I live next door!'

The tall girl was peeping down curiously from the first floor landing and looked amazed when she saw who was below. 'Leila!' she gasped. 'What on earth are you doing here?'

'I thought you'd come to see me and arrived at the wrong house. I've just moved in next door. Don't say you're my neighbour?'

Both girls collapsed into laughter as they had done so often in their student days. Dee dragged her up the stairs. 'Let's talk. I'll put the kettle on.'

Leila was already experiencing severe pangs of conscience. She'd deliberately neglected to keep in touch with Dee, except for postcards or brief letters from around the world, but had often found long, newsy letters from her friend waiting on her rare visits home.

Dee had been with her on that holiday in Cornwall when she first met Lance, and had told her bluntly that she was an idiot to jump into bed with him almost at once, and even more of an idiot to rush off with him to Hawaii. What she would have said if she'd known who was footing the bills Leila hadn't stopped to find out.

She'd never admitted that only six weeks later she had her suspicions that Dee had been right, and after three months had been sure of it. Why hadn't she finished with Lance then, instead of letting it drag on? If she'd done that he might still be alive.

As if knowing her thoughts, Dee said, 'I read about Lance, Leila. I'm sorry.'

'Thanks. I'll tell you about it, later.' Leila glanced around the flat. It was furnished comfortably with Dee's flair for colour and design, and she wondered if Dee lived there alone. Then she noticed the broad wedding ring, topped by a small square emerald.

'Dee! You're married!'

The other girl smiled. 'Don't look so astounded! I'm surprised you didn't know because you were invited to the wedding.' She looked Leila straight in the eye. 'As a matter of fact I asked you to be my bridesmaid, but apparently the letter never reached you. Nobody knew exactly where you were.'

Appalled, Leila stared at her, and then to her own acute dismay burst into tears. She flopped down limply on a kitchen chair. What else would she find she'd missed while whizzing round the world with Lance?

Hard, painful sobs tore at her chest, and the more she tried to control herself the more violently she wept. Through her tears she saw the shock and astonishment

on Dee's face before her friend enfolded her in warm
comforting arms.

The XJS roared effortlessly along the motorway. It was
a Monday morning two days before the competition
deadline, and Leila was about to visit the site for the
fourth time. All she needed there was half-an-hour in
which to take a few last-minute photographs and to
reassess the stretch of water which she was transforming
on paper—into a boating lake. In black Levis and a
cream sweater she had a no-nonsense air about her, and
looked even more businesslike when she put on her
heavy-duty wellies.

She turned to leave the car and stopped dead. The
hitherto quiet site had become a scene of purposeful
activity. Workmen were everywhere. The group of
deserted huts had doubled in size, a residential caravan
was parked nearby and men were manoeuvring earth-
moving equipment across the stretch of mud leading
from the road.

All this made its impact on Leila, but her astounded
gaze switched back to the huge, three-sided notice on its
triangular stand. White lettering a foot high on a dull
blue background: 'Parnell Enterprises'.

She hovered uncertainly by the car while it registered
that Matt had landed the contract for the leisure centre.
So—what should she do now? She could hardly march
all over the place taking pictures without explaining her
motives, and she hadn't the slightest intention of doing
that!

Vague plans to return in the evening and sneak past
the night-watchman chased each other across her mind.
She was edging back towards the car door when a shrill
whistle from the cabin of an enormous crane halted her.
'Hi there, bonnie lass!' A beefy, weather-beaten face
looked out, wreathed in smiles, and she beamed with
pleasure to see her old friend. 'Ben!'

The man who climbed down from the cab was a
Garland workman who had known her since she was a
child. Leila went up to him and shook his calloused hand.
'Ben—it's lovely to see you. Are any of the others here?'

'Not today, lassie.' The Geordie accent was there for all time. 'I'm the only Garland fella here, because I'm handling the big stuff.' He took off the yellow hard hat and ran a hand through his wiry grey hair. 'Er—I'm right sorry about the boss. You'd be away, I reckon, when it happened?'

'Yes,' she said gently. 'Ben—are you quite happy with Mr Parnell? And the lads—they're all in work?'

'Aye.' He smiled and nodded. 'We're all in work—and glad of it, I can tell you. The boss is here somewhere—the new boss, that is.'

She looked round quickly. 'Oh, I thought he went round in a Range Rover. I don't see it.'

Ben shook his head. 'Oh, it's a helicopter he's using.' He waved a hand in the direction of the playing fields. 'Over there somewhere. If you want him I'll send a young lad——'

'No,' she said quickly. 'No. I have no business with Mr Parnell, just as I had nothing to do with the takeover. In spite of it being Dad's firm I never really knew much about the business side of it, you know.'

'Aye. We all know that, sure enough. I'd better get on, then. The lads are waiting.' With a nod he plonked his protective headgear back in place and climbed up to his cab.

'Good morning,' said a deep, familiar voice behind her.

She whirled round. Matt was on the steps of the caravan, wearing cords and a checked shirt. She smiled uneasily, recollections of their last encounter making her feel awkward and self-conscious. 'Oh—hello, Matt.'

'Satisfied?' he asked, straight-faced.

'What?'

'Are you satisfied? With the way they're being treated? What are you aiming to do, visit each site in turn?'

'W-what?' Lord, had she lost her wits as well as her voice?

'I don't imagine you've come over here for a pleasant country drive, so I take it you're playing detective. You were questioning the crane-driver and I know he's one of the Garland men.'

'I wasn't exactly questioning him,' she protested. 'It's Ben, I've known him for years. I just saw him—or rather he saw me—and well——'

'You just saw him as you happened to be passing on your way to the South of France,' he said deliberately. 'Wearing the footgear that's so popular on the Riviera this season.'

She stared at him and moistened her lips. Was this the gentle, unruffled man she'd known in Hawaii? She gathered a few remnants of self-possession and said crisply, 'I suppose technically I'm trespassing, aren't I? No, I wasn't passing on my way to the South of France or anywhere else in particular, but I *was* in the area and thought I'd just look at the site.' For the fourth time, she added silently. 'I believe a big leisure centre is going to be built here and I see that Parnell's have landed the contract. Congratulations.'

'Thanks.' His eyes were still hostile.

'Well—I'll be going.' A pity I ever came.

He looked surprised. 'Oh. Perhaps—you'd like a cup of tea? There's always tea available on building sites, but of course you know that.'

She nodded. 'Yes. But I won't bother, thanks.'

'Leila.' He stretched out a hand as if to detain her. 'Are you feeling all right now?'

Oh great! Back to the personal stuff just as if he hadn't been as awkward as hell. Still—he *had* asked. 'I'm all right,' she answered with a faint smile. 'Goodbye, Matt.'

She left him standing on the steps of the caravan and was thankful that he hadn't been near enough to the car to spot her notebook and camera, or worse still, the site plans spread over the back seat. She started the car and whirled away with a disdainful roar of the engine, realising too late that she could hardly feel the pedals through the heavy wellies, and wondering why she had an odd little ache beneath her ribs.

'Sam tells me you're still burning the midnight oil.' Dee dumped a box of groceries on Leila's table. 'Don't expect me to keep on doing your shopping once your entry's in, you know. And what's more we expect a flat-warming dinner as well when you're a lady of leisure again; cooked—we're prepared to risk it—by your own fair hand.'

Leila looked at the pile of drawings and dye line prints on the floor, and yawned widely. 'It's almost ready for tomorrow. You've been an angel, Dee, and as you've invited yourselves I've no option but to give you a meal very soon; cooked, at great personal risk, by myself.'

Dee dropped a kiss on top of her head. 'The risk,' she said, laughing, 'will be all ours! See you later.'

'How did Sam know I was burning the midnight oil?' asked Leila seriously.

'He was called out to the hospital last night, got back at three a.m. and saw your lights still on. Leila, you're putting all you've got into this Cowper thing. You're not going to be all shattered if—well—if——'

'If I don't win? No—I don't expect to. You know we spent six months of real slogging on our degree designs and I've spent barely a month on this. But I had to try. It's so exactly my sort of thing—you know I always liked the big sites. To be honest I feel pretty pleased to have managed anything constructive at all. Quite a change, for me.'

She saw Dee watching her closely, but since that first afternoon there had been no more tears. Then, she had wept for so long that Dee had tried to get Sam from the hospital, convinced that it was some sort of mental breakdown. At last Leila had calmed down, and bit by bit told her friend about what had happened in Australia, about her return home to learn the news of the takeover, and about Arlene deciding to sell the house. She'd even confided in Dee about her J.T. Rose entry for the competition. As for Matt, she'd mentioned meeting him in Hawaii, that was all. The episode on the beach at dawn was locked away neatly in one of the cupboards of her mind.

Sam had worked late that night, and arrived home at 11 p.m. to find them both still deep in conversation, with Leila looking an absolute wreck after weeping for so long. She, in her turn, had been eager to meet the man who had led her friend so speedily to the altar, and who figured in almost every sentence she uttered. Leila knew he was from Dee's home town, that he was several years older than her, that he was highly intelligent and a registrar at the big hospital nearby.

That gave her a clear mental image before she even met him. He would be tall, to match Dee's streamlined five foot ten; studious as befitted his brains, and remembering Dee's previous taste in menfriends he would be quiet and restrained.

She knew she was wrong when a voice bellowed from the doorway, 'Dee—licious, Dee—lightful. Where are you?' A stocky, thick-necked fellow bounded into the room, stopped dead on seeing Leila, said, 'Hello there,' and then went across to his wife and kissed her very thoroughly, almost standing on tiptoe to do it.

Leila tried not to show her astonishment. Dee had never previously looked at any man under six foot, but Sam couldn't be more than five-six, and he was halfway bald into the bargain. He released his wife and then took stock of Leila while Dee introduced them. She saw that his eyes were startlingly blue and very direct; literally the one redeeming feature in a very ordinary face. What had he got to attract Dee? Lovely, elegant Dee with her bright brown hair and slanting hazel eyes, her flair for clothes and her brilliant wit?

'Hello, Leila,' he said gently. 'Glad to have you with us. Dee's told me a lot about you. We were sorry you couldn't make it to the wedding. How long can you stay?'

Gracious and welcoming words from a man who had come home looking all set to toss his wife into bed, and instead found her deep in talk with a friend he'd never even met.

'I'm not staying with you and Dee, Sam. I live next door—in the top floor flat.'

After that they all shared a late supper; Leila thrilled to see Dee so happy and still slightly puzzled as to what she saw in Sam.

Two days later Dee spelled it out for her as they

shared a coffee. 'It's what's inside the parcel that matters, not the wrapping,' she said with a laugh. 'You're too polite to say but you wonder what I see in him. He has the most attractive personality and the most interesting mind of any man I've ever known. He's completely unselfish and he's absolutely marvellous in bed. I adore him, Leila.'

Now Leila rolled up her designs. 'If I thought our degree work was gruelling I'm at a loss to describe my efforts during the last month,' she said wearily. 'At least I can catch up on my sleep now.'

'You've checked that you've got J.T. Rose on each and every copy?' asked Dee.

'Yes, it's all OK. Three hours to the deadline—talk about cutting it fine! Still, if anything ghastly happens like the car breaking down, I'll have time to take it in by taxi.'

An hour later Leila entered the Cowper rooms to find the same elderly clerk in charge. He took her entry, signed a receipt and presented it to her with a surprising little flourish.

She walked down Waterloo Street in bright May sunshine feeling almost light-headed with relief at having met the deadline. She wasn't entirely happy with her design; shortage of time had meant that certain aspects had lacked the very detailed work they cried out for, but on the whole it wasn't bad. She'd managed to incorporate a few of the daring innovations which she enjoyed dreaming up.

Traffic roared past as she approached the Council House. With a little lift of the heart she turned the corner and headed for the Art Gallery. The fountains were sparkling and a fresh breeze was blowing the spray towards her. Life suddenly seemed good. If working on the Cowper competition had done nothing else it had brought some of the savour back to living.

She ran up the steps and gave the doorman a brilliant smile. Moments later she was wandering through the galleries searching for her favourite pictures as one seeking old friends. There were several that she particularly liked but, as always, she was compelled to stand for minutes on end before the Pisarro study of the Bridge at Rouen. She loved it.

She left the gallery refreshed in spirit but un-imaginably weary in the flesh. She would go back to the flat, have a long warm bath and then go to bed.

CHAPTER FIVE

'THAT was a meal to remember, Leila.' Sam spoke with a straight face, and again she glimpsed something of what Dee saw in him. Several times lately she had been brushed by the warm aura of their love, and each time had felt an unwelcome envy grip her heart.

Sam was certainly different from Dee's earlier men. His formidable brainpower was concealed behind a boisterous personality and a sharp but never unkind wit. Stocky, bald, short-sighted he might be, but already Leila barely noticed his appearance.

His comments on her meal were typical. He hadn't said it was delicious, because of course it hadn't been; he'd said it was a meal to remember. She knew quite well that the steak had been overdone, the french-fries soggy and the coffee meringue distinctly chewy. But Dee and Sam were fine company, the wine was good and the cheese excellent.

'Next time I'll take you both out for a meal,' she said gloomily as they drank their coffee. 'My natural aptitude for cooking is nil.'

'Oh, not quite as low as that,' said Dee, grinning. 'You just need more practice. And speaking of natural aptitude, you've got plenty for interior decor—the flat's beginning to look terrific.'

Leila eyed the different levels of the room with affection. Shaggy rugs in white or dark green left most of the broad golden floorboards bare, and the varied woods of her favourite pieces of furniture from Ardenfields added the stamp of her own personality and taste. The low seating units covered in leaf-green linen were from her rooms at home, as was the big oak desk and all her drawing equipment by the rear window.

'I've enjoyed working on it since I finished the Cowper thing,' she admitted. 'If I end up with a job miles away it will be an awful wrench to leave it.'

Dee watched her thoughtfully, and then said, 'You know my boss, Wilkinson?' Leila nodded, all attention. Dee worked in the landscaping department of one of the local authorities. 'You remember I was telling you he's pretty good on large-site work? Well, he told me today that he's one of the judges for Cowper. I mentioned that a close friend of mine has entered, and also a few other people I know, and he said that as soon as a decision is made he can tell me who's won as long as I don't make it public.' Dee hesitated, looked at Sam, then said, 'Do you want me to tell you or would you rather wait to be notified?'

'Oh—you tell me!' said Leila at once. 'It might save me twenty-four hours of waiting. And don't look so agonised. I'm not seriously expecting to win, you know. In fact, since I found out that Matt Parnell's firms are the builders I think it might be easier in some ways if I never set foot on the site again. He was an absolute horror when he thought I was checking up on how he's treating the Garland men.'

Dee's lovely hazel eyes were still watchful. 'Do you know any more about his firm?' she asked. 'And what about him? Is he married?'

Leila stared at her. It seemed mad but she had no idea whether he was or not. She recalled that on the little island she'd fallen fast asleep instead of showing the basic courtesy of polite interest in his business and his family.

'I don't know,' she said slowly, and faint colour tinged the skin over her cheekbones. 'He could be, I suppose, although he seemed without any ties when we met in Hawaii.' The woman in the beach-buggy with him that day, though? Was she just a friend? 'Did you say you fancied the late movie on the box?' she asked hurriedly, collecting the coffee cups.

It was a week later when Dee called on her way home from work. Leila had just got back from a visit to Ardenfields where Arlene had complained about the lack of prospective customers for the house. Dee looked hot and slightly rumpled—unusual for her. She avoided

Leila's eyes and accepted a weak gin and lime with a strained smile.

Leila breathed in deeply. 'All right, you needn't tell me. I can guess. Who's won?'

'I must be transparent,' sighed Dee, relieved. 'It's some chap up in Cumbria—a freelance. But Leila—you came joint second.'

'Joint second! Who with?'

'Wait for it. Digby Jones.'

If Leila had felt remotely like laughing she would have guffawed. They both knew Digby. A fellow student on their course, he was brash, assertive and horribly confident. He was also a good designer. The Cowper judges had known their stuff where he was concerned.

She dredged up a smile. 'I might as well have come fiftieth as second. They need only one design after all. At least I can be thankful I shan't be called upon to work in harness with Digby.'

Dee finished her drink. 'I'm sorry, love, but I have to dash. Sam's working this evening so we're eating at six. Are you sure you're OK?'

Leila leaned forward and planted a kiss on her cheek. 'I'm fine. Tomorrow I'll start job-hunting.'

Dee went off looking dubious, leaving Leila guilty at her own eagerness to be alone. Suddenly the flat seemed empty and echoing, and she went aimlessly to the window and sat in the leather chair that had been her father's. Outside a blackbird was singing in the chestnut tree. Pure, effortless song, liquid and unforced, reminding her of Ardenfields and the little grove of birches by the stream. There had always been birdsong there.

She realised that far from being shattered at not winning she was delighted at coming second. After eleven non-creative months she'd worked hard and produced something of merit. It seemed to put her glamorous, unhappy wanderings with Lance into a kind of perspective—reducing them to a bitter but educational episode in the course of her life.

Relentlessly she travelled through the past, walking

with careful, sober tread the paths she had first sped along barefoot. Her infatuation with Lance, those early weeks of passion and desire, with the times of uncertainty and misgiving becoming ever more frequent. Her father, trying desperately to understand, accepting her farewells with a smile and a kiss. She didn't spare herself the memory of that last Christmas, her first ever away from home, spent on the burning, brassy beaches of Australia because Lance refused to go to Ardenfields, and to have returned without him would have been to admit that it had all been wrong, that it was over.

The golden haze of summer faded over the rooftops of the city, but still she sat on, her mind selecting images for inspection, examining each one and then bringing forward the next. Two funerals ... two in a month, and each with its burden of shock and remorse ...

It was quite dark when she stood up. She felt stiff as a board and hungry as an adolescent, so she had a quick shower and put on clean jeans and a loose muslin shirt. Restlessly she hovered in the kitchen, trying to decide what to eat, then with a toss of the head she grabbed a sweater and her car keys and a moment later drove off towards Hagley Road.

She attracted a few glances as she ate at a table for one in a restaurant still crowded, although it was after eleven. Slender, golden-skinned, her immense dark eyes ringed with faint shadows, she seemed oblivious of the curious stares and projected an image of reserve and fragility. Fragile or no, she ate an enormous meal, but drank only Perrier. Night driving in the XJS demanded a clear head.

She walked out of the restaurant purposefully, having known since she left the flat what she was going to do next. Switching on the engine, she headed for the Cowper development. What better time to bid it a silent farewell than at midnight under a full moon? She would have felt a fool doing any such thing in broad daylight, but the warm anonymity of darkness gave her the courage to be sentimental.

She stopped the car quickly some distance from the

site and walked down the slope of the approach road.
The three great oaks fluttered their leaves with weary
dignity as a faint breeze passed, and beyond them the
water gleamed fitfully beneath the willows.

Leila stopped by the fence. Work on the site had still
hardly begun, apart from digging the footings and the
inevitable channelling for pipe-ways. A nightwatch-
man's hut, snug and silent, was by the gate, and was
that music she could hear?

She edged further along the fence, by now cross with
herself for coming and skulking around in the dark, and
surprised that she'd let the overgrown site get to her the
way it had. She soon realised that the music was coming
from the big caravan where she'd seen Matt Parnell that
day three weeks ago. She moved along and saw dim
lamplight through the windows. Was he *living* in it?

She could hear the music clearly now; it was Brahms,
one of the symphonies. It seemed to her strange and
rather unnerving to hear the controlled thunder of
Brahms on a deserted building site at midnight, with
only a night-watchman and a towering circle of
bulldozers for audience.

She stood there as if bewitched, until the symphony
came to an end and she saw the figure of a man rise
from a seat in the lamplight and move into the depths
of the caravan. It was Matt.

Abruptly she realised her position, standing peering
over a building site fence at dead of night. Quietly she
turned away and went back through the shadows aware
for the second time of that strange little ache beneath
her ribs.

The insistent ringing of the doorbell dragged her from
sleep the next morning. It was eleven o'clock! She
grabbed her robe and whirled down the spiral staircase,
remembering that it had been three a.m. before she'd
climbed it to go to bed.

The bell rang again and she smoothed her hair before
opening the door. A man stood there in a dark suit,
immaculate shirt and tie and holding a briefcase. A
mop of brown hair curled tightly over his head and

confident dark eyes looked her up and down. 'Is Mr
Rose at home? Mr J.T. Rose?'

She could have groaned. He was from Cowper, and
here she was still in her robe at eleven in the morning.
'Come in,' she said quietly. 'It's me you want. I'm J.T.
Rose.'

The man ran a hand over the abundant curls without
seeming to realise he was doing it, and the gesture rang
a small bell of memory. Where had she seen him? But
he was over the threshold with a sort of leap and was
right behind her as she led him to a seat. 'Please sit
down,' she said. 'I'm afraid I was still asleep when you
rang the bell. I was very late last night——'

The alert eyes watched her every move as she sat
opposite him and she in her turn noted the dull sheen of
fine worsted in his suit, the gleam of gold at his cuffs,
the silk shirt and tie. She hoped he'd get to the point
quickly if he was going to tell her she'd come second,
and wondered if she should admit that she already
knew.

He bounced to his feet again. 'My name is Robin
Cowper—of the Cowper Foundation. You haven't seen
your mail this morning, Miss Rose? It is *Miss* Rose?'
His glance flicked to her fingers and as quickly away
again.

'I haven't been downstairs to collect it yet. Why, did
you have news for me?'

He smiled with considerable charm and an obvious
knowledge of how to use it. 'Congratulations, Miss
Rose. You've won first prize in our Landscape Design
competition!'

If he expected astonishment he wasn't disappointed.
'*Won* it?' Leila felt her cheeks go cold as colour left
them. 'But I don't think—that is—how——'

'You'll know as soon as you open your mail that you
weren't actually first choice,' admitted Robin Cowper
ruefully. 'The committee have been up half the night
making phone calls and arguing. Yesterday we sent
letters to all the runners-up and a telegram to the
winner. As he lives in Cumbria we asked for verification
of his Midlands birth in order to fulfil the terms of the

bequest—we thought of it as a mere formality. That's where the trouble began. He rang back to say he'd bring in his birth certificate in person—it stated that he was born in South Cheshire.'

He sat down again and stared at her, his well-cut curls starting to look a trifle wild and woolly. She waited, outwardly calm, as he went on, 'He really believed that being born in that part of Cheshire entitled him to enter, but the Foundation couldn't agree. We've had to disqualify him—*not* a happy experience for either side, needless to say. That led us to the joint winners of second place—yourself and a Mr Digby Jones.'

'Joint winners,' Leila repeated dutifully, as if it was the first she'd heard of it. Inwardly she shuddered— she'd have to work with Digby ...

Robin Cowper jumped up and loped across the room. With a flourish he whirled round on her. 'We were faced with the prospect of our joint second-prize winners working together when their designs were entirely different. We contacted Mr Jones first thing this morning, to find that he's just signed a contract to work in Saudi Arabia. So I'm here to tell you it's all yours. Congratulations, I've come hot-foot in person as I couldn't get you on the phone.' He swivelled his head from side to side as if unable to credit that there was no telephone in the flat.

'I'm still waiting for it to be installed,' explained Leila.

He ignored that. 'Please, *please* don't tell me you're currently working in Edinburgh and were born in Istanbul.'

She smiled with a touch of restraint. He was a bit overpowering. 'No, don't worry. I was born in Birmingham and I live here now.' She crossed to the drawers where she kept her documents. 'Here's my birth certificate.'

He held out his hand. 'Great! So what does the J.T. stand for? No—let me guess—Juliet, of course ... Juliet Titania—how's that for a Shakespearean double?'

'Just a minute,' she put in hastily. 'The J.T. Rose is

just a pseudonym.' All at once she was uncertain about whether such a thing had been allowed. 'I hope that doesn't mean you'll disqualify me as well.'

He looked carefully at her birth certificate. 'Leila Garland,' he said consideringly, 'a pity—I could have called you Rosie. Well, it's OK. Pseudonyms are accepted. Can you come back with me now? A working party is standing by to meet you.'

She stared at him. 'But how did you know you'd find me in? Surely they aren't waiting there on the off-chance of you taking me back?'

'No, not really. It's the weekly get-together of all our key people; architects, surveyors, builders, the Cowper financial wizards and anybody else who's useful.' He stood there, impatiently shifting his weight from one foot to the other.

'Perhaps I could offer you coffee while I get ready?' she asked. He accepted, then sat back, opened the briefcase and took out the *Financial Times*.

Twenty minutes after he first rang the door-bell, they left the flat together; Leila outwardly cool and self-possessed in a dolman-sleeved dress of ivory cotton. He led her to a red Aston Martin—a V.8. Vantage, and she concealed a smile—a Cowper would hardly drive around in a Mini! She eyed the instrument panel, impressed. It was more like an aircraft than a car.

He drove the magnificent car with the restless energy which had so far characterised his every action; crouched over the wheel, revving impatiently at each hold-up, tooting a melodious horn at unwary pedestrians and tossing snippets of information at her almost non-stop.

'Call me Rob,' he instructed when she addressed him as Mr Cowper. 'I can't stand the name Robin—it's only suitable for under-fives. "Christopher Robin is saying his prayers"—ugh!'

Leila clutched her seat as they sped round a corner but he continued his briefing on the Foundation without a pause. 'Old Howard B, the original millionaire, was my grandfather. His children are my father, my uncle and my aunt. Between them they administer what's left of the money after about five hundred charities have had their whack.'

It was somehow endearing to hear him talking so openly of the Cowper millions. 'Various uncles, aunts and cousins hang around,' he went on, 'as financiers, accountants and so on. I qualified in company law with the idea of making myself useful and if possible indispensable. All the key positions are kept in the family, you see.'

The Cowpers were no family of idle jet-setters, thought Leila. Howard B's money might provide them with a luxurious lifestyle, but at least they worked for it. She found herself watching him, fascinated yet slightly repelled. Seen in profile his face was typically English, clear-skinned and lean; but when he turned towards her the broad, high cheekbones and full-lipped mouth gave him a foreign, almost Slav appearance. His eyes, confident and assessing, looked into hers far too often for a man driving a powerful car in heavy traffic, but his behaviour towards her was scrupulously correct. Odd, she could have sworn that a pass was imminent the moment they seated themselves in the car.

He zoomed below street level to a car-park under an office block behind Colmore Row; left the car at the entrance and tossed the keys to an eager attendant, then led her briskly to the Cowper rooms. It was noisy and very hot, with brilliant noonday sun killing any shade from the buildings, but indoors all was quiet and orderly. The same clock ticked the peaceful minutes away; the same elderly clerk rose to greet them from behind his highly-polished counter. It seemed to her an inappropriate background for Rob Cowper; glass, chrome and concrete would have suited his personality better than mahogany and Victorian figured glass.

A moment later they were outside double doors on the third floor. 'Right?' he asked encouragingly. A little push from behind, a warm hand on her arm, a flourish and: 'Ladies and gentlemen, may I present Miss Rose, our Landscape Designer.'

There was a full minute of silence, all eyes on Leila, followed by subdued murmurs around the table. Then they all began to talk at once as she was introduced. Afterwards, she could recall ten of them, eight men and two women, but the events of the next half-hour remained out of sequence in her mind like random snapshots of a hurried business trip. The way Rob announced her by the J.T. Rose pseudonym threw her completely; that and the sight of Matt Parnell, cold-eyed and wary after a first stare of undisguised amazement.

Much later she admitted to herself that Rob had been right to use that name. The group of people waiting there had already seen two finalists eliminated from the winners, and were expecting J.T. Rose to be a man. Oh, she had known at once what that awkward silence signified; astonishment and dismay that she was a woman. Looking back she could see that it would only have made things worse if, after presenting her when they all expected a man, he had introduced her by a name that none of them knew. None of them except Matt Parnell.

'It was utterly gruesome,' she said that evening in Dee's flat, sipping celebratory champagne bought hurriedly by Sam at the local off-licence. 'There was Rob Cowper, all bounce and bonhomie, while everyone else looked sick at the sight of me.'

'Including your friend Parnell?' asked Dee shrewdly.

'Oh, he looked astonished, and then livid,' admitted Leila.

'But weren't there any other women there?' Sam was intrigued.

'Two. Both members of the clan, I think. One was elderly, wearing little half-specs and a twin-set; I think she's secretary to the Bequest Committee. The other was a financial consultant. She was gorgeous—black hair, creamy skin, turquoise eyes.'

'Turquoise?' Dee sounded sceptical.

'Blue-green, aquamarine, like sea over golden sand—turquoise. They were lovely and so was she. *And* she has a brain *and* she can use it. I think she's Rob's cousin.' Leila yawned widely. It had been a hectic day.

'Honestly, Leila,' said Dee, sounding like a proud

parent with a brilliant offspring, 'I do think it's marvellous. You've landed the design job of a lifetime, it's exactly on your wavelength, and you're mixing with millionaires right, left and centre.'

'I don't know if any of them are actually millionaires *now*,' said Leila, yawning again. 'But they're all loaded. Christopher Robin drives a brand new Aston Martin, and Turquoise-Eyes was wearing a diamond the size of a pea on a platinum chain round her neck. The architect was a misery, which might make things difficult. He looked daggers when Rob presented me like a ringmaster with a high-wire act.' She smiled suddenly. 'High-wire act—very apt. I expect that's what it'll feel like with Matt Parnell and the architect on one side, the Cowper family on the other and me trying to keep my balance in the middle. Why didn't I look for a cosy little number with a local authority?'

Dee poured them all another glass of champagne and absently plonked a kiss on Sam's shiny head. 'Because you're destined for higher things, that's why. You know you were always the girl wonder on the course. And you can stay on in the flat, as well.'

'Yes,' said Leila, 'though I shall miss you both like anything if you move away.'

'When, not if,' said Sam gently. 'It's either general practice and a house in the country or the final grind towards a consultancy at the hospital with a house nearby. We've got to decide which, haven't we, love?' He gave Dee a look of such tenderness that Leila averted her eyes, feeling an intruder. 'Either way,' he concluded, 'we'll be moving within the year.'

Leila smiled at them both, outwardly at ease. 'I'll just have to keep my fingers crossed that you stay in this area, won't I?' she said lightly.

Soon afterwards she left them and went back next door with Sam's final remark lying like a stone in her heart. She was embarked on a very demanding career, surrounded by strangers who could well prove hostile, and the only people who cared if she failed or succeeded, lived or died, were three elderly servants and Dee and Sam. If they moved away she would be on her own. Birmingham was a big city and she knew many people there—but not one of them intimately.

She climbed the stairs to her flat, her back very straight and her chin high. It would soon be Monday. It was time to look forward—she'd finished looking back.

CHAPTER SIX

LEILA slept badly the night before she was due to start work. She was nervous, and as if to underline her tension a spectacular thunderstorm raged over Birmingham.

Not a good omen, she decided, lying there watching the lightning and trying to ignore the din of a violent electrical storm. The rain was so torrential that she envisaged the site being like a sea of mud.

Restlessly her mind went back over the last few days. There had been a meeting with the architect, Martin Deeds, a thin-faced redhead who exuded contempt, something which didn't surprise her. She'd come across other architects who regarded landscape designers as unnecessary interfering busybodies. Many architects did their own landscaping and usually the ones who didn't believed their buildings to be so magnificent that the surrounding land was quite unimportant.

And she had lunched with Rob Cowper at the Albany. Christopher Robin, as she still thought of him, had been pushy, but pleasant and correct. It was probably her own edginess that had led her to expect a pass every time he opened his mouth.

Then there had been a rather fraught session with the Bequest Committee and several key people in the Foundation. Perhaps she'd been too optimistic in imagining that she'd already won full approval for her design. After all, if they'd thought it without a fault then presumably they would have awarded it first prize. Whatever their motives, they put her through a kind of third-degree which made the three-hour session a gruelling ordeal.

Only Rob backed her, not from any knowledge of landscape design, she felt sure, but because he fancied her. His behaviour might be restrained, but the look in his eyes was only too easy to read. His energy and

70

optimism had been no match, though, for Martin
Deeds and his ally, Larkin, the site-agent for Parnells.

The body of Cowper men were more concerned with
safeguarding the terms of the Bequest than with
anything too technical, but there were several professional men present, and she could tell that Deeds and
Larkin had made their views known before she arrived.

The architect had protested that her plans for a
raised terrace linking the indoor and outdoor swimming
pools invaded his own province of building design. He
dug in his heels and insisted that the terrace was
removed from the plan.

After that, one question followed another. The
outdoor sports specialist queried her siting of the tennis
courts and finally Larkin announced that her earth-
shaping proposals were a little late as building
foundations were already being laid.

Quiet, controlled, Leila prepared to do battle. 'But
surely you realised that any competent landscaper
would want *some* earth-moving? Wasn't it rather rash
of you to start on the foundations before the winning
design was examined?' Earth-shaping was one of her
special talents; hadn't she lived it and breathed it
throughout her teens, given it extra time and study on
her course? Point by point she went through the plans,
checking elevations, depths of top-soil, positions of
drains and culverts.

At last, silence fell on the men bending over the
tables. 'Well—perhaps,' conceded Deeds grudgingly.

'Let it go, then,' agreed Larkin. 'I'll tell Mr Parnell
we've been into it all in detail.'

Leila longed to ask if Matt had backed them or even
dreamed up their proposals himself, but she kept quiet
and concealed her satisfaction at winning the battle. She
saw Rob looking across at her, then he closed one dark
eye in a conspiratorial wink.

Thunder crashed, lightning speared the darkness,
while Leila recalled the meeting in minute detail. Surely
her sex hadn't been the reason for all the niggling, the
fault finding? She hadn't the slightest proof of any such
prejudice. Only instinct guided her. Nobody had said a

word about her being a woman, but she hadn't missed the sudden flash of Martin Deeds' glasses and his stare when she started on the technicalities of the flow of the main culvert, or Larkin's disgust at having to give way about the earth-shaping. It was instinct which told her that there had been more behind his attitude than a natural resentment at being thwarted.

But why? Her design had been accepted, hadn't it? As second-best admittedly, but it had been chosen by men who knew their jobs. Wearily she reviewed the landscaping profession. Of course women were gaining degrees in it every year, and other qualifications as well, but she didn't know of one working on a large site comparable to Cowper's. Schemes of that size were still almost exclusively a male preserve. Their attitude could only mean that they resented having a woman on the job.

It was some time later, while rain still drummed on the roof, that she wondered for the first time if perhaps they had reservations about her because of her lack of experience. Deeds and Larkin were probably in their forties; one a qualified architect, the other a civil engineer. Was it really so surprising if they were wary of a landscape designer who hadn't even worked since gaining her degree? Wouldn't they have felt just the same if she'd been a man?

With a sigh at her own blindness, Leila gave her pillow a final thump. She must guard against imagining that her being a woman was behind every criticism or complaint. 'Do the job,' she told herself. 'Do it with all your skill, energy and judgment. After a week nobody will even notice whether you're male or female.'

With that she turned over and fell fast asleep, while overhead the thunder rolled reluctantly into the distance and the first rays of sun cleaved the departing clouds.

At the stroke of eight that morning she parked the XJS and crossed the quagmire outside the gate of the site. She was unfettered by rules and with nothing laid down about her hours of work, but she could hardly wait to get started.

Men were already busy pumping out flooded trenches or extricating equipment from the mud. Some of them glanced at her curiously but didn't ask what she wanted. It was possible they couldn't even tell she was a woman. In wellingtons, jeans, cotton shirt and a straight denim jacket, and with her hair top-knotted under a hard hat, she looked like a slender teenage boy because the clothes she wore concealed the outline of her breasts and hips.

She had decided that her first priority must be to examine the areas where earth-levels were to be altered and then ensure that the work would be carried out.

She clumped across the site, astonished at the weight of her heavy-duty wellies when, after only a moment, they became clogged with mud. She soon found that by stepping from one tussock of grass to the next she missed the hollows in between and was less likely to get bogged down, and made her way to the stretch of water to assess the slight natural slope of the land. Her plans for the sloping banks would have to wait until the cleaning and dredging had been done, and the sluices installed to keep the water fresh. She pulled out her notebook and carefully jotted down ideas to which she could give thought later, when she was back at the flat.

The sensation of being observed made her turn and there, following her, was the unmistakable figure of Matt Parnell. In spite of all her resolves she felt her shoulders stiffen defensively. Guilt still plagued her about not telling him she'd entered the competition.

He came within two paces of her, and she saw that already he had a smear of oil on his chin and streaks of mud on his shirt. She waited for him to speak. If he was pleasant then she would be the same. His beautiful mouth softened briefly. 'Leila,' was all he said in greeting.

'Matt,' she replied non-committally. 'Good morning.'

'We like new arrivals at the site to make themselves known, not to go wandering about at will,' he said evenly. 'Larkin and I were expecting you, but not quite so early.'

'Oh!' How could she have forgotten such an

elementary courtesy? Fool. 'I'm sorry, Matt. It wasn't deliberate. I just didn't think of it.' She was put out to find herself apologising in the first five minutes.

He nodded again, then said: 'I didn't get the chance to say much the other day at the Cowper rooms, but my congratulations.'

If ever there was a suitable moment to explain about her secrecy, this was it. But his manner didn't encourage confessions or apologies. He was polite, mildly pleasant, but he was distant. Edgily she let the opportunity pass and said nothing beyond an awkward 'Thanks.' If he mentioned the competition later she would explain then.

'If you'd like to come back with me I'll show you your office.'

She looked up. The morning sun was behind him, etching his face and hair darkly against the sky. Only the eyes were unchanged; grey, level, and at that moment distinctly chilly. She wriggled her shoulders, but answered brightly enough. 'I didn't expect an office. In fact I envisaged keeping all my stuff in the car.'

He walked at a leisurely pace, his long legs covering the sodden turf easily, while she slipped and slithered in an effort to keep pace with him, her feet feeling as if they each weighed a ton. He stared down and waited, an odd expression on his face, but made no attempt to assist her. For that she was grateful; the last thing she needed was the boss helping her along as if she was a wilting Victorian miss. But he had one suggestion to make.

'Wouldn't you be more comfortable in wellies that are less heavy? The sort you're wearing are fine for men but I should have thought——'

'I'm used to them,' she said swiftly. 'I've worn them before, you know.'

'For a full day?' he asked mildly.

'Well, perhaps not,' she conceded, 'but for several hours at a stretch.'

He shrugged. 'Just a suggestion, that's all.'

They were back at the hub of things near the main entrance and Matt began to explain the uses of the various huts. They looked inside the canteen; a long, low building filled with tables and chairs, backed by a kitchen where a grizzled old man rattled pots and pans. 'The meals aren't bad,' said Matt. 'The days when navvies used to fry eggs on their spades are over, as I'm sure you know. Jacob is an ex-navvy—his food's rough but very enjoyable.'

Past two identical huts next; small, neat and painted in dull blue like the canteen and the big Parnell sign. Notices on their doors said, *Martin Deeds: Architect* and *Peter Larkin: Site Agent*. 'Pete Larkin's always around somewhere,' said Matt, 'but Deeds is only here occasionally.'

They then came to his caravan. It was modern, spacious, and the same blue as the huts. 'Parnell's colour,' he said, reading her thoughts accurately. 'I live here for a few days at a time if things are hectic. I often do that in the early stages of establishing a site, and I visit the others by helicopter. The caravan's my office and I take my meals here. Larkin also has his meals over in his place, and I want you to do the same with yours. The men need to relax completely in their canteen, you see.'

She nodded in agreement. 'They'd feel a bit awkward if I went in there, I realise that.'

'So might you,' he said drily, 'if you heard their language.'

She looked at him curiously. In some ways he was surprisingly old-fashioned. Lance and his friends had used four-letter words as everyday speech. At times it had irritated her but she quickly became used to it. 'That wouldn't bother me,' she said.

'Maybe not, but it would me. And the men wouldn't be at ease. Keep out of the canteen at all times, Leila. Now, to your place.'

They moved on and arrived at a little rustic cabin made of logs set at the far side of the main gate. It was charming, with a big picture window shaded by a wooden verandah, and was so different from the plain Parnell huts that she viewed it with astonishment. But she said nothing, not even when she saw the hand-painted sign by the door, *Miss J.T. Rose: Landscape Designer*.

Matt unlocked it and they stepped inside. It was well-equipped for an office, but for a building-site hut it was positively luxurious. The walls were lined with pale pine boarding, there was a pine workbench, a drawing board, a swivel chair and two leather-covered easy chairs. There was even a calor-gas cooker and full crockery cupboard. Matt pointed to the rear door. 'Your own individual toilet block,' he said. 'I take it you don't want to share *that* with the men?'

'No, of course I don't,' she agreed. 'I *had* been wondering about it, I admit.' She looked round the cabin and felt deeply uneasy. 'Matt, what's the idea of all this? It's lovely, and thanks a lot, but it's not necessary. I don't expect fuss—special treatment—luxury even, just because I'm a woman. What on earth made you do it?'

That odd expression was there again, a sort of baffled look. She glimpsed it before his eyelids came down. 'I didn't,' he said flatly. 'Left to me you would have got a blue Parnell hut with a table and chair and the little loo at the back.'

She took off the hat, and her thick silky hair, escaping from its top-knot, fell down to her shoulders. Absently she twirled it up again and pushed in a few pins to hold it. It gave her a most comforting sensation of relief to hear that he hadn't been so insensitive as to lay on the luxurious cabin for her. 'I'm glad it wasn't you,' she said impulsively. 'But—it was Cowpers, then?'

'Robin Cowper in person. The cabin came Friday morning. It was fitted up in the afternoon, and the rest of the stuff came on Saturday.' He gazed out of the window. 'I refused the carpet. Sent it back to the shop.'

Leila felt a strong desire to giggle. Rob Cowper didn't know much about building-sites, that was evident. Then annoyance took over. Had he no *sense*? Here she was, determined that within a week everyone would have forgotten she was a woman while he was busy making sure they all remembered.

'He's mad,' she said shortly. 'I shall feel an absolute

fool using this place.' She saw the sceptical expression still on Matt's face and it seemed to her that the high-bridged nose was lifted in a very unbelieving manner.

'It isn't my doing, you know,' she said rashly. 'There's no need to look as if there's a nasty smell beneath your nose.'

'Nasty smell?' he repeated with infuriating calm. 'Far from it. You smell delicious, as always. I didn't imagine for a moment that it was your doing, although having seen the two of you together I certainly thought it was Cowper's.' He looked towards the cupboard. 'Has he provided you with a vase?'

She looked at him blankly. 'A vase?'

'For the flowers. When they arrive. As I'm sure they will before long. The Cowpers of this world always send flowers, don't they?'

'I wouldn't know,' retorted Leila coldly. 'I've never had dealings with the Cowpers of this world until now.'

'Really?' He walked to the door, then detached her key from a huge bundle and laid it on the worktop. 'I'll send a lad to unload your gear from the car, then when you've settled in perhaps you'd come across to the caravan and we'll discuss plans for the coming week. Ten o'clock.'

With that he walked rapidly way. There had been no 'Will that suit you?' or 'Is that convenient?' she noticed. It had been an order. On this site there was one boss—Matt Parnell.

A small white van stopped outside the gate as she turned to go back inside the cabin. Matt strolled across to it and she saw him look across at her. The driver got out and looked dubiously at the sea of mud, and as if taking pity on him, Matt took hold of the long florist's box and came back to her, carrying it with exaggerated care.

He put it into her unwilling arms while she clamped her jaws tight shut. Fury made her cheeks burn and her eyes smart; fury with Rob Cowper as well as the man in front of her. 'I'm sure you'll find a vase there somewhere,' he said smoothly. 'See you later.'

Seething, she rushed inside, hoping none of the men

had seen. Helplessly she looked at the great sheaf of roses; long-stemmed, creamy, perfect. She fought and overcame the urge to go out and throw them on the vast pile of rubble near the bulldozers.

The card was addressed to Miss J.T. Rose, and on it was written in a large, flamboyant hand: *Welcome to Cowper's. Have a good day. Rob.*

Pete Larkin opened the door of Matt's caravan. Oh great! she thought. The day had begun badly and looked like continuing in the same way if she had him to deal with as well as Matt. Light-blue eyes observed her, cool and hostile. It was the first time she'd seen him as a separate person rather than half of the Deeds-Larkin duo. Unlike the architect, he was thick-set and beefy, with the weather-beaten complexion common to so many building-site workers. 'Good morning,' she said, scrupulously polite. He returned the greeting civilly enough and departed, leaving the two of them together.

'Sit down, Leila. Pete's been telling me the results of your little contest with him and Deeds about the earth-moving. You won, I hear. Pretty good going—they're both very experienced men.'

'So I gathered. I might have won that particular point but I had to give way on several others. Did he tell you that?'

He held up a sheet of paper. 'Yes, Pete's nothing if not efficient. He runs the site when I'm not here. Don't let his manner upset you, it's just that he's a bit wary of amateurs.'

'But I'm not an amateur,' Leila pointed out tensely. 'I might be lacking in experience, but I have professional qualifications.'

He sighed. 'Sorry, sorry. A tactless slip of the tongue. It remains, though, that for Larkin you *are* an amateur, whether it's an accurate description or not. Time will perhaps prove him wrong, let's hope so. Now—I've jotted down several points. First—are we to leave the name plate on your office as it stands, or are you reverting to your own name?'

'My own name,' she said promptly. 'Rob Cowper

knows that perfectly well. I can't think why he insists on using the other one. Besides, most of the Garland men who work for you know my real name. It will seem mad if they have to use another one.'

'A rose by any other name,' he quoted, allowing the shadow of a smile to touch his mouth. 'We could tell them you'd decided to keep to the J.T. Rose for professional reasons.'

She hesitated. There was one quite compelling reason for using her own name and she might as well admit it. 'I think my father would have been pleased to see a Garland on site,' she said quietly. 'That's the real reason, Matt.'

'Right,' he agreed gently, and all at once she saw in his eyes the warmth and understanding she'd known so briefly in Hawaii. She was hardly aware that her own eyes shone with sudden tears; she forgot her determination to keep free of involvement with him, and before she knew it she was talking, gabbling almost, the words spilling over each other in her eagerness to say them. 'Matt—about the competition. I feel so awful about keeping it all secret and telling you that stuff about going to France or Italy or wherever it was.'

'Well, why did you?' he asked reasonably.

'I told myself it was because the name Garland is well-known in the trade. I didn't think I'd win and I didn't want a Garland to be a loser. It seemed absolutely vital at the time that nobody should know. I was mixed up and unhappy, and the competition was what I needed to get myself back to normal. It seemed a sort of—of goal——' Her voice trailed off and she bit her lip. Oh dear, what a rigmarole. No wonder he looked bewildered.

For a moment he stared at her in silence and she was reminded of their time on the coral island, when he had listened to her as they lay on that glistening sand. She realised that he had the gift of concentrating his whole attention on whatever was being said to him, and the fanciful idea came to her that if the caravan collapsed about their ears, he would still lean towards her, intent and deeply interested.

'If it was a "sort of goal",' he said, 'then you've achieved it, haven't you?'

'Yes, I suppose I have. But I'm surprised by it and a bit overwhelmed, you know. It's the first time in my life I've worked—the first time I've earned my living, that is. Mad, isn't it, at twenty-five? The events of the last few days have shown me that it isn't going to be easy though.'

'Easy? Who wants life easy?' he asked. 'If you struggle for something and finally achieve it surely it means more to you than if it falls into your lap without effort?'

She found herself nodding. What he said was so obvious, so true, it made her worries about the job seem unreal and a trifle neurotic.

'One last question,' he said, 'and then we get down to business.' The phone rang. He stretched out a hand, lifted the receiver, and without bothering to find out who was calling, said briskly, 'Ring again in ten minutes.'

She was intrigued. 'Suppose it was something vital.'

He shrugged. 'If it's all that vital they'll ring again before ten minutes are up. You said a moment ago that when you entered the competition you were mixed up and unhappy. "Were"—the past tense. Does that mean you're not unhappy any longer?' He was watching her intently.

She considered the question, knowing quite well that she was very different now from the tense, guilt-ridden woman who had gone to Hawaii. Even so, she couldn't blithely dismiss the leaden remorse which still weighted her down, still haunted her dreams.

Beyond his shoulders she could see a gang of workmen unloading bags of cement. She watched them for a moment, her too-bright eyes enormous in the smooth golden oval of her face. 'I'm still a bit mixed up,' she admitted at last, 'still a bit unhappy. But it's getting better all the time. Thanks, Matt.'

And then he smiled. It really was the most devastating smile she'd ever seen; probably, she told herself, because it was so *rare*. 'I'm glad,' was all he said.

Then he crossed behind her chair to where the caravan wall was covered in designs and detailed blow-ups of Martin Deed's'building plans. Her own design was there; just the small-scale plan of the whole site. They stood side by side, each in stockinged feet, with the top of Leila's head just below the line of his shoulders.

'Have you brought all your own copies of your design with you?' he asked. 'Good! I'd like you to do me a new one, devoted solely to the earth-shaping. One plan—large scale—all the earth-shaping in detail. Can you manage that?'

'Of course,' she said stoically. 'How soon?'

'Wednesday morning. Until then we'll be laying the main drain here ... and here ... and putting in the footings of the main buildings and the pools.' A long finger touched the plan between areas shaded in blue.

She looked at it carefully. 'But you've already shaded in the areas scheduled for re-shaping,' she said, puzzled. 'Do you want it done in more detail?'

'Oh yes,' he said decisively. 'I only marked that from memory. I want earth levels laid down in *exact* detail. With luck, your ideas won't affect what we've already done. The only foundations we've started are the ones for the main hall, and that's so massive the level is inevitably that of the basic bed-rock. Next—the alterations you've agreed to with Deeds—the terrace, etc. I'd like the full set of your plans adjusted accordingly as soon as you can. When you've done them all, put them in sequence on the walls of your office. Right?'

'Right,' she said, mentally bracing herself for at least seven or eight days of detailed work.

'Finally, the water. I'm arranging for a specialist firm to send someone to discuss the dredging and cleaning, so that it can be put under way in time to make ready for autumn planting. Will you be available some time this week to talk to the chap when he comes, along with Larkin and me?'

'Yes.' She had the sensation of being swept along by a gale-force wind. What was more she felt sure she hadn't made a remark of more than one syllable for at least five minutes. This was the other side of Matt Parnell. Dynamic, decisive, a bit ruthless.

There was a knock on the door and the old man from the canteen came in with two mugs of coffee on a tin lid. 'Leila—meet Jacob, our site cook. This is Miss Garland in charge of landscaping.'

They shook hands ceremoniously. Jacob's face was seamed and pitted, his white hair cropped almost to the scalp. Small bright eyes watched her warily, then he turned to the door. 'Don't let it go cold,' he said to Matt, with a nod at the coffee. He darted a final glance at Leila and gave a quite audible sniff. Leila smiled ruefully. Jacob and Agnes might be poles apart but they had a few things in common.

The coffee was hot, strong and delicious. Leila sipped hers and wondered if Matt had dealt with all the items on his list. The phone rang again and this time he listened. 'Speaking . . . oh, hello . . . yes, I was busy . . . no, that's OK . . . of course . . . I can leave here at five . . . Right, see you then.'

His telephone manner was nothing if not brief and to the point, she thought. 'Is there anything else, Matt?'

'No, that's all for now. Let either Pete Larkin or me know if there's anything you need. Oh—a phone will be laid on for you tomorrow.' He shot her a blandly innocent look. 'As far as I know it will be just an ordinary one—not black onyx or gold-plated or anything like that——'

She finished her coffee and went to the door. Take it lightly, she warned herself. 'By the way, you were quite right about the flower-vase,' she said sweetly. 'There was one in the cupboard. Cut crystal, and just *lovely* for the roses.'

CHAPTER SEVEN

'I'M shattered,' admitted Leila, reclining on one of the settees that were her belated wedding present to Dee and Sam. 'It was humiliating really. By lunch-time I could hardly drag one leg after the other through the mud. My back was sore, my head ached and I'd have given anything for a cold shower.'

Dee counted stitches with what seemed to Leila to be obsessive care. She was knitting a cricket pullover for Sam, who played for the hospital term. 'You're bound to find it tough at first,' she said comfortingly.

'I know, but my legs felt as if they were about to drop off at the hips, so in the lunch hour I drove to the shops and bought myself some lightweight wellies. Three pairs. Pink, yellow and blue.'

Dee looked up at that. 'Three pairs?' she said incredulously. 'They sound a bit—dare I say it—feminine.'

'I know,' agreed Leila morosely. 'But what are pastel-shaded wellies compared to ye olde log cabin and a crystal vase overflowing with long-stemmed roses?'

'You didn't tell me that!' squealed Dee. 'Rob Cowper sent you *flowers*? To the *site*? In a *vase*? Then he does fancy you. I knew it.'

'Yes,' said Leila, 'but don't get excited, it's not mutual. No, the flowers didn't arrive *in* the vase. That was just there, waiting, in the cupboard. When I see him I shall have to tell him I don't like it.'

'You can't do that! In any case, I thought you liked crystal.'

'Dumbo! I mean I shall have to tell him I don't like all the fuss. I feel an absolute idiot in that luxurious cabin and Peter Larkin positively sneered at it this afternoon.

'And what about Matt Parnell?' asked Dee. 'Did he "positively sneer" as well?'

83

'Yes he did, as a matter of fact. And he told me to get some lightweight wellies, so he'll think I've rushed to do his bidding. But I think he'll be all right to work with, or rather work *for*. A bit of a slave-driver though, given half a chance.' Then she added, 'He's going around with Turquoise-Eyes.'

'What, the financial wizard? Well, well.'

'She rang Matt up this morning and then called at the site for him at five o'clock. He strolled out of his caravan looking like Mr Universe in tennis-gear.'

'Well, well,' said Dee again. 'You're not going already?'

'I've got work to do on the plans,' said Leila, smiling rather wearily. 'There's more to this earning a living than meets the eye, it seems to me. I say, Dee, Turquoise-Eyes was on Hawaii.'

'You saw her there?'

'Yes. It dawned on me where I'd seen her before when she came to the site with her hair up and wearing big sun-specs. That's how she looked when I saw her in a beach-buggy with Matt the day I flew home.'

'Well, well,' said Dee for the third time.

The motorway was already busy as Leila drove to the site early next morning. She'd been awake since five thinking about the railway embankment beyond the tennis-courts, but had been unable to check her design as that particular sheet was still in her cabin. She moved over to the exit-lane, slowing down with her eyes on the road and half her mind on the site.

The energy she'd felt when she jumped out of bed evaporated rapidly as she approached it. Deeds and Larkin were right—she couldn't handle it. She'd taken on more than she could cope with. All right, so she didn't carry sole responsibility—Martin Deeds and Matt did that, with Larkin as second string, but she had to fulfil the promise of her designs and the knowledge of what that entailed lay like lead across her slender shoulders.

Before she switched off the engine she could hear the harsh clatter of an aircraft overhead. Matt's blue-and-white helicopter was about to touch down on the playing-fields. Some game of tennis, she thought wryly; more like a night-long session with Turquoise-Eyes.

She felt a little self-conscious, arriving at seven o'clock and was relieved to find the site still deserted. As she unlocked the door of the cabin her heart lifted at the scent of new wood and leather, two of her favourite smells. All at once the luxurious surroundings seemed less unreal and out-of-place than they had the previous day. Something in her that was purely feminine acknowledged that it was good to be in such a well-appointed office, instead of a Parnell hut with just a table and chair. From her window she saw Matt making for his caravan: he looked remarkably at ease for a man who was badly in need of a shave and wearing full evening dress at seven in the morning.

Leila raised her eyebrows; the latest working gear for the successful builder, perhaps? She spread out plans on her work-bench and fastened the one she'd brought with her to the drawing board, then started on the intricacies of earth-shaping around the subsidiary buildings.

At nine-thirty she made herself coffee and was drinking it at the work-bench when she saw Ben, the ex-Garland crane-driver, go past her window carrying a huge mug of tea towards one of the earth-movers. She ran to the door and called him, 'Ben—how lovely to see you. Come in for a minute.'

The grey-haired Tynesider halted facing her, but came no nearer. 'My, Miss Leila, but the lads are right pleased to have a Garland on site again. We weren't expecting you, though, because of the name on your door. It was only when Shorty saw you going in the boss's caravan yesterday that we knew you were here.'

'Oh, that,' she waved at the name-plate, 'it's just a name I used for entering the landscaping competition. It's going to be altered very soon. Won't you come in and have your tea with me?'

He shuffled his feet. 'Well, no, the boss might not like it.'

Leila brought her coffee cup and sat on the step. 'Sit

here for a minute then, or do you want to get back to your mates?'

'Nay, bonnie lass. It's just that the boss says we mustn't bother you. No whistling after you, no swearing when you're around, no talking, even, not to you, that is.' He took a drink and wiped his mouth with the back of his hand.

Leila stared at him, half-amused. She'd known him since she was a child and he wasn't to be allowed to talk to her? 'I don't think Mr Parnell meant you, Ben. He probably doesn't know you're an old friend.'

'What the boss says, goes,' he told her, unconvinced. 'But we're right glad you're doing the fancy stuff on the site. Your Dad would ha' been proud.'

The unpredictable tears stung her eyes as he went on his way. Most things left her dry-eyed, but the unexpected kind word could bring on the tears. He was right. Her father would have been proud to see her on site 'doing the fancy stuff', having won the job on her merits.

She watched Ben as he leaned against his cab, tea mug in hand, eating an enormous sandwich. It would have been good to talk to him for just a few minutes. She looked across at Matt's caravan, her lips jutting ominously.

Later that morning she was intrigued to find duckboards being put down across the worst of the mud. After hours of wrenching her feet in and out of sodden ground it was almost like walking on air to tread the firm boards when she went to see the foundations of the main building to check on the sub-soil. As she returned, the sound of a powerful engine caused her to look towards the main gate. Rob Cowper was there, parking his Aston Martin.

Cringing mentally, she edged back to her cabin. The last thing she needed was him around making a fuss of her. He hadn't spotted her, so with interest she lingered to see how he negotiated the duckboards in his Gucci shoes.

Typically he walked with as much aplomb as if he

was strolling through Chamberlain Square. He looked round, then ignored Matt's caravan and made for her cabin, smiling when he stopped by the open door. 'Hello, there! I've come to take you out to lunch.'

Leila looked at him coolly. 'I'm sorry, Rob. I eat a snack lunch here on the site. In any case I'm not dressed to go out anywhere.'

The confident dark eyes flicked up and then down, assessing her slim form. She was wearing a yellow cotton shirt with her blue jeans and her hair was piled up beneath the hard hat which was compulsory wear for all workers out on the site. He grinned easily. 'You didn't arrive in all that gear, did you?' he asked. 'Go and change, there's a good girl. I'll wait.'

'Of course I arrived in this gear,' she said. 'These are my working clothes.'

'Oh, my God,' he said in disgust. 'You don't *have* to wear them surely?'

'I do if I'm to be comfortable,' she said evenly. 'This is a building site, not a fashion show. And while we're on the subject, I believe you're responsible for this office and its furnishings?'

He looked round, smiling with a touch of complacency. 'Yes—I planned it myself. What do you think of it?'

'It's comfortable and convenient and I appreciate your—your kindness. But I have to tell you that this cabin is out of place here. It's ostentatious and far too luxurious, and I wish you hadn't done it.'

He stared at her in stupefied silence. 'What's more,' she went on, 'the flowers you sent embarrassed me terribly. Please don't do anything else to make me feel conspicuous.'

'But most girls would——' he began.

'I'm not "most girls",' she interrupted quietly. 'I'm me. And as I recall it there's nothing in my contract to say that I must allow myself to be embarrassed on this site by any member of the Cowper family who chooses to make a fuss of me. I don't like it, Rob.'

His mouth tightened. 'You'd prefer a—a *hut*? Like those over there?'

She hesitated, caught off-guard. She wasn't at all sure that she *would* prefer a bare Parnell hut to her luxurious cabin.

Rob didn't miss her hesitation. 'Come on, Juliet, the truth.'

She bit her lip. 'This cabin is comfortable and good to work in. But it's made me feel conspicuous and emphasised that I'm a woman among the men.'

'And that needs emphasising?' he asked derisively.

'Oh, come on. I apologise, though. I just saw it as a little gesture of welcome, that's all.'

It wasn't easy, to stay annoyed when he stood there on the floor of the little gesture, smiling and completely unrepentant. 'Well, so long as you remember in future,' she said weakly.

At that her wrists were caught in a surprisingly strong grip as he leaned forward and kissed her firmly on the mouth. It wasn't entirely unexpected, but she felt as violated as if he'd attempted the most intimate caress. No man had touched her lips since Lance, and she recalled all too vividly that this last kiss had been devoid of any tenderness.

Rob smelt expensively clean and his lips hovered, warm and full, expecting response. When she gave none he let her go. 'All right,' he said, 'I get the message. No touching you here on the site. No fuss on the site. No——'

She felt rather than saw the shadow in the doorway and whirled round to see Matt there. He looked big and rather grubby next to the immaculate younger man, his face and hair dark against the sun-bright sky. 'When you've finished here, Leila,' he said, 'come over to the caravan, will you?' He walked away without waiting for a reply.

Rob stared after him with more than a hint of smugness in his expression, while Leila scanned the site in front of the cabin. If any of the men had seen that little scene! She sank limply into the armchair and eyed Rob with distaste; how could she ever have found him likeable? 'You've got the message?' she said icily. 'Not all of it, apparently. It's this: no touching me on site, no

fuss on site, *or anywhere else*. I won that competition on
the merits of my design, right?'

'Right,' he agreed.

'I owe you no favours, right?'

'As before,' he said tightly.

'Then leave me alone,' she said shortly. Brown eyes
glacial, she met his gaze. 'I don't want you here, Rob. I
have a job to do. Leave me to get on with it.'

'You don't understand, Juliet.' His voice was velvet-
smooth. 'I always get what I want.'

'Not this time,' she said. 'And the name is Leila. Leila
Garland. I'm having the name-plate altered.'

She saw faint colour rise beneath the broad
cheekbones, then he shrugged, and without another
word strolled nonchalantly away across the boards. She
saw him head for Matt's caravan, where the two of
them conferred in the doorway for a moment. Then,
still at a leisurely pace, he made for the gate and his car.

She would have liked to postpone the talk with Matt,
but he'd said: 'When you've finished here, come to the
caravan.' What did he imagine she needed to finish? A
passionate love scene?

Hat removed, she found herself releasing her hair and
combing it, then examining her face closely. Suddenly
still, she stared accusingly back at herself in the mirror.
Why the sudden urge to check on her appearance?
Uneasily she let her mind run on a track other than that
of the job, and seriously considered her emotional state.

For someone determined to stay uninvolved with any
man she had landed herself in a strange situation—the
only girl among a hundred men. It would be no
hardship, though, to stay uninvolved with Rob. He was
a pain.

But that one little kiss had set off its own chain of
physical reactions. All at once she was acutely aware of
the men around her. Rob's kiss had left her
unresponsive, but she could still feel his lips, still smell
the expensive cologne, still see the smooth angle of his
jaw. Equally she was aware of Peter Larkin striding
over a mound of excavated earth a hundred yards away
as he directed the bulldozers. She could see his

powerful, stocky form as clearly as if he was beside her, his weathered skin, hard blue eyes and grey-streaked hair.

As for the man she must now go and see, images of him whirled around her mind. His gaze, clear and grey as he watched her and Rob from the doorway; his body, tanned and heavy with muscle as he crossed that Hawaiian beach towards her; his hands, firm and impersonal as he towelled her dry, and that astonishing smile when they talked together in his caravan the previous day ... Heavens, what was wrong with her? She grabbed a notebook and pencil and made for the door.

Shirt tucked in neatly, wearing flat shoes for once instead of her wellies, she walked sedately along the duck-boards. It felt good to have the sun on her hair; she wasn't yet accustomed to covering it with protective headgear all the time.

Matt was speaking on the phone at his desk by the window. He waved her in and pointed to a chair as he finished his conversation in the brisk incisive manner she'd noticed before. He hung up, then swung his chair round to face her.

The first thing that registered was the lack of expression on his face. He was annoyed, she thought. He was going to be unpleasant. She found her jaws aching from being clamped together too tightly, something which often happened to her under stress. Consciously she relaxed and sat there, outwardly calm, waiting to hear what he had to say.

It came as a surprise when words seemed lost to him. His gaze wandered absently over her face, her hair, her lips, but he remained silent. Then he opened his lips to speak, but changed his mind. After a moment he shook his head slightly and said, 'I want to discuss a few points about the boating lake before the chaps come to see us on Friday.'

'Oh,' she said flatly. It was a bit of an anti-climax after nerving herself for a scene.

'You sound surprised,' he said drily.

At that, irritation flared in her. He knew perfectly

well that she was surprised, and why. 'I was expecting
you to be unpleasant about Rob Cowper kissing me,'
she said steadily, finding a perverse pleasure in bringing
it into the open.

'Unpleasant?' he repeated, as if that was a word
which could never be applied to him in a thousand
years. 'Why unpleasant? You're a grown woman, he's a
grown man—or so I've been led to believe. If he's
helped you forget your sorrow over your boyfriend then
I'm glad.'

She gaped at him, speechless, and he went on. 'But as
you've mentioned the matter, I admit I'd prefer it if you
could both save the amorous interludes for elsewhere. I
don't want the men distracted.'

'There won't *be* any amorous interludes, in private or
in public,' she said tightly. 'What you saw was—
unexpected. At least to me.'

'That isn't the version Cowper gave me before he
left,' said Matt briskly.

'Maybe not but it's the version that happens to be
true. I owe Rob Cowper nothing. I got the job on my
merits, not because of him. I don't want him here when
I'm trying to work, and I've told him to leave me
alone.'

He leaned forward intently. 'Is that so?' There was a
look on his face, not disbelief, but what? Scepticism?
Wariness? Before she knew it she was replying to his
earlier remark. 'And he doesn't make me forget about
Lance, either.'

Black lashes dropped, shutter-like, concealing what
the clear eyes might have revealed. 'No, of course not.
Sorry.'

It was hardly the time or the place to explain the
intricacies of her feelings about Lance, but she had one
more thing to clear up. 'Ben Ford, on the heavy plant,
tells me you've forbidden the men to have anything to
do with me. Why is that?'

He sighed audibly. 'Because you're one woman
among a lot of men,' he said patiently. 'Some of them
are pretty rough types.'

'But I've known the Garland men for years!'

'I daresay, but I can't have half of them chatting you up and the rest not allowed to speak to you. It's got to be all or nothing. So—it's nothing.'

Nothing . . . She swallowed painfully, her throat dry. Nothing. It was impossible to tell him she felt in desperate need of a friendly word, an encouraging remark. If she aimed to be treated as an equal of the men how could she whine that she was lonely and a bit scared into the bargain?

He took her silence as a protest. 'I'm sorry, Leila, but I've worked on building sites for almost twenty years and I could count on one hand the women I've seen on site in that time. Most of my men are decent. A few aren't. I employ them for their working skills, not their chivalry. You're very attractive, beautiful in fact, and whether you believe it or not you're potential dynamite on the site. Here, what I say goes, and I say you keep a low profile and don't encourage any familiarity from the men. And that's final.'

He hadn't raised his voice or spoken sharply but she recognised the note of authority. She found herself nodding wordlessly in agreement. Then he stood up and added abruptly. 'That means no more clinches with the Cowper heir on my site.'

It was too much for Leila. She turned on her heel and left the caravan. If he wanted to speak about work let him come to her.

She marched back across the boards to her cabin and, snatching up her plans and her drawing gear, bundled them all together. She would go back to the flat and work there, free from distractions. A moment later she roared off in the XJS with quite unnecessary noise, and was half way home when she remembered that Matt had said she was beautiful.

'Huh!' she said aloud, and zoomed on along the motorway.

By mid-evening she was feeling better. Working at home had its drawbacks as well as its advantages, though. The special plan for Matt was almost finished but she still needed two sets of measurements which could only be obtained by checking the foundations which were already dug against those on her own plans.

Frustrated, she stared out at the chestnut trees. Oh, great! Either she must go back now to the site or be late in submitting the completed plan to Matt. Her pride decreed that he must have it first thing. 'Wednesday morning' he had said—so he would have it at eight a.m. if the effort of doing it reduced her to jelly.

Taking her notebook and measures she set off back to the site. Surely at this time it would be deserted except for Charlie, the night-watchman? As for the boss, doubtless he would be giving his evening clothes another airing—at least she sincerely hoped so.

As she approached the site she began to have misgivings about her abrupt departure earlier in the day. She'd steamed off like an overwrought prima donna because Matt had annoyed her. Ruefully she reviewed the events of the morning. She'd better watch it in future if she didn't want to be labelled as a temperamental female.

Charlie looked up from his evening paper and called to her affably as she passed his hut, otherwise the site seemed deserted. The scent of newly dug earth hung on the still air and somewhere a thrush spilled out his evening song. Quickly she went to where mounds of excavated earth marked the foundations of the swimming baths. No duckboards here, she thought ruefully, scrambling on hands and knees.

She couldn't help thinking that evenings were a good time to examine, without an audience, what was being done on site. Her quick eye could pick out which foundations belonged to the various parts of future buildings, and as always she was impressed by the speed and accuracy of the work. By chance she had been there when the foreman jotted down a set of measurements on a grubby scrap of paper, and here was the result, accurate to a centimetre.

At last, satisfied she'd got what she came for, she turned to climb back. There above her, his back to the darkening sky, was Pete Larkin, looking anything but pleased to see her. 'Oh, Mr Larkin. I had to come back to take a few measurements for my plan of the earth-levels. Mr Parnell wants it in detail by tomorrow morning.'

'Oh yes.' As usual, he sounded civil but unforthcoming.

'Yes.' Sparkling conversation, thought Leila. And what was he doing here so late? Had he no home to go to?

'Miss Rose,' he said, 'or Miss Garland, whatever you wish to call yourself. Don't you realise that we can't have you wandering about here on your own so late in the evening?'

'But I'm doing no harm. I'm accustomed to building sites. And my name is Garland. The name Rose was just a pseudonym I used for the competition.'

He looked at her and said heavily, 'I'm not thinking of you *doing* harm but of *coming* to harm. If you should hurt yourself or have any sort of accident and Charlie didn't know, you could lie here for hours. Matt wouldn't like that.' The choice of words implied that though Matt wouldn't like it, he himself would remain unmoved if she lay injured all night long.

Leila kept silent and thought rapidly. It would bring her no advantage whatsoever to be constantly at loggerheads with Larkin, because if he so chose he could put stumbling blocks in her path every hour of the day. She resolved to swallow her pride, and dredged up a smile. 'I spoke to Charlie as I came in,' she said pleasantly, 'and of course I wouldn't wander about the site on my own if nobody knew I was here, but thanks, anyway.'

The hard eyes widened slightly and he waited while she joined him. 'Thought I'd better spell it out, just in case,' he said awkwardly.

'I want to do a bit more work when I get back, so I'll say good night, Mr Larkin.'

'I'm off as well.' He trudged at her side with the easy, tireless tread of a man used to rough heavy ground.

'You're here late yourself,' she ventured amiably. 'Do you have far to travel?'

'Solihull,' he said shortly. 'I haven't much—that is—I'm in no hurry.'

At the car she turned to him and smiled. 'Good night again.' She bent down and changed her footgear. He didn't reply and was still standing by the gate when she looked back through the mirror. A bulky, thick-set man in black cords and a checked shirt. Something about the solitary figure touched off a small fount of sympathy in her. *He* looked lonely as well.

CHAPTER EIGHT

IT was a plaintive letter from the family lawyers. Mr Dobbs had tried for weeks past to contact Leila regarding her father's will. Probably, she thought, because he knew she hadn't been listening when he read it after the funeral. He'd written to her in Scotland, Australia, the south of France and Hawaii, he said, and had rung Ardenfields regularly to check on her whereabouts. Now that he'd at last been given her correct address, would she contact him at once regarding the terms of her father's will? The precise wording of the letter conjured up a picture of Mr Dobbs, with his disapproving manner and scrawny red neck.

Leila sat at the breakfast table and faced the prospect of seeing him again. It had been quite beyond her to take in the contents of the will after her father's funeral, and two weeks later, when she was still numb with grief, Lance had made such an issue of it that she had dug in her heels and flatly refused to contact the lawyers. That had led to their last bitter quarrel, and the quarrel had led to Lance's death . . .

Sighing, she pushed the letter into the pocket of her clean jeans and resolved to ring Mr Dobbs later that day. For the present she had other things to think about.

She poured herself another cup of coffee and sat down again for a moment. The last two days had been busy. True to her resolve she had presented Matt with the completed plan at eight o'clock on Wednesday morning. She had found him already at his desk, deep in papers, and whether or not he realised how hard she had worked there was no way of knowing. He thanked her, pinned up the large sheet on the wall and said: 'I'll study this for a day or two then you can have it back for a while to get some dye lines done from it.'

She was about to go when he said, 'I'd still like a word with you about the boating lake before Friday.' No mention of her abrupt departure the previous day, then? Somewhat relieved, she agreed to a discussion late the next afternoon when he came back from a trip round the other sites.

After that all had been tranquil for two whole days. She had worked steadily on the revising of her designs; used her newly installed telephone with an unfamiliar sense of pride; had her name-plate altered at last, and seen nothing at all of Rob Cowper.

Apparently the boss's word was law about chatting her up, and she found she could go about her business on the site without it being emphasised that she was a woman, and different. She was answered pleasantly and politely if she asked anything about work, otherwise a brief greeting was all that was offered. What was more, Pete Larkin had spoken to her twice, not only civilly but almost affably. She found herself humming as she pinned a new sheet on her drawing-board.

Outside the cabin the smell of damp earth was overlaid by diesel fumes from the heavy machinery. Men were shouting, engines revving, cement-mixers chugging. She looked out and saw a scene of organised chaos.

It was at that moment, a set-square in her hand, a pile of drawings waiting to be altered, the coffee-pot on the stove behind her, that Leila felt content. It was a sensation that had escaped her for almost a year. The last time she could recall feeling real contentment had been when she gained her degree in landscaping. Then, her future had been taking shape ... work on the Garland sites, and perhaps in time a partnership in the firm. She had joked with her father about it being 'George Garland and Daughter'. Everything had seemed so right, so satisfying, until she chanced on that remote Cornish beach and met Lance ...

She worked on her plans until late, waiting for Matt's return. All the men had gone home. It was uncannily quiet, until the clatter of a helicopter ripped through the silence.

Minutes later he came across and stood in the doorway, one hand up against the frame, looking tired and a bit irritable. Black beard-growth shadowed his jaw and his shirt was torn from shoulder to buttons, revealing congealed blood mingled with the tight dark hair on his chest. 'You're still here then?' He sounded surprised. Had he forgotten he'd asked her to wait for him?

'Yes, still here. As I've been for eleven hours so far today. I thought I'd better hang on for a while as you'd asked me specially.' She eyed his chest uneasily. 'You seem to be in need of first aid.'

'Oh, it's not as bad as it looks. Some fool on the new roadworks tried to move me out of the way in a hurry with a J.C.B.' He lifted his mouth ruefully. 'He almost succeeded too.'

She stared at him. Being accidentally shifted by one of the giant diggers could have been dangerous, even fatal. But he didn't seem to want a fuss. 'You're building a road, then?' she asked with interest.

'Just a stretch of dual carriageway for a town by-pass,' he said briefly. 'I'm sorry I've kept you waiting, Leila. I hoped to ring you but I was too tied up. Are you in a hurry to get away?'

'No,' she said, and all at once it was true. The urge to get home had disappeared.

'Give me ten minutes to shave and change, then come across, will you?' He looked at her for a minute, taking in the sun-streaked hair pinned up loosely on the crown of her head and escaping now in tendrils round her face. His eyes flicked to the drawing-board, and then to the piled-up designs on her work-top. She imagined that his mouth softened for an instant, then he ran a grubby hand over the thick black hair and went back to the caravan.

She took across a fresh pot of coffee. After all, he'd looked as if he could do with some. She tapped on the open door and heard him call to her to come in, so she made for the tiny kitchen and put the coffee-pot to keep warm. It was very clean and neat, like a ship's galley; in fact the whole big caravan put her in mind of a boat.

Matt came out of the bathroom, dressed in clean denims but without a shirt. His hair was still damp and she saw that it curled wetly against his neck. Heavens, she must be staring like a goggle-eyed adolescent, but if he went round displaying that impressive chest . . .

'It took a bit longer than I thought to get it clean,' he said, dabbing bloodstained gauze at the gash. 'Does it look all right to you?'

Her legs moved slowly, heavily, as if they were made of lead, obeying her subconscious objective to keep well away from him. In that instant she knew she'd been right in thinking she was becoming sexually aware again. Panic gripped her. She wasn't yet ready for it. Uncertainly she hovered in front of him.

'Come on, Leila,' he said impatiently. 'Do I look like a sex maniac? I remember the first time we met you treated me like a potential rapist. All I'm asking you to do is look at this scratch to see if it needs any more swabbing.'

Leila went scarlet. She could hardly explain that she was scared of her own reactions rather than his. Meekly, she went close to him and peered at the ugly gash on his chest. He spelt of antiseptic, of soap and peppermint toothpaste. At least she was to be spared exotic male perfume. 'I can see what looks like specks of rust,' she said uncertainly. 'Would they be from the J.C.B.?'

'Probably,' he said wearily. 'Get 'em out, if you can. The first-aid box is in the bathroom.'

She found it in the still steamy little room. 'Do you want to come in here?' she called, adding antiseptic to warm water in the wash-basin. He strolled in and she saw that the tiny, functional space was barely big enough to accommodate them both.

He stood at her side and looked down. 'Relax,' he said gently. 'I've never yet tried for a girl on the rebound and I'm not starting now. I'll leave that to Cowper.'

Gently she probed with the swabs, appalled at the dirt still embedded there. 'Rebound?' she repeated, without looking up.

'It's still only eighteen weeks, isn't it?'

Amazed, she raised her enormous eyes to his, the gibe about Rob forgotten. *She* knew it was eighteen weeks since Lance died, because the remorseless calendar in her mind crossed off the days and weeks, and never let her forget them. But that *he* should know it!

'Yes, it's about that,' she acknowledged quietly.

For a while they were silent; she delicately swabbing the wound, Matt staring studiously over her head. She found it an intimate and oddly disturbing confrontation. At last she leaned away and brushed damp hair from her forehead. 'It looks much better now, but the edges need holding tightly together if it's to heal. Have you any steri-strips?'

He rummaged in the box and found a new pack, but still she hesitated. 'They'll get all tangled up with the hairs,' she pointed out.

'Cut them off, then,' he said easily. 'There's some scissors.'

Carefully she trimmed the curly black hairs on either side of the gash. Her face was so close to his chest she imagined she could hear his heartbeat, regular but surprisingly rapid. She pressed the sides of the gash together and fastened the strong sterile strips across it. Unconsciously she sighed with relief when she'd finished.

He took hold of her hand and held it tightly in his warm hard grasp. 'Thanks, Leila. You don't like hairy chests, do you? I'm sorry about that.'

She jumped guiltily. It wasn't so very long since she'd thought so, too. 'Not at all,' she protested. 'I don't mind in the least.' But he was still holding her hand. Uneasily, she wiggled her fingers to remind him, and he let go at once. 'Can I get you a drink?' she asked.

'Of what?'

'I've made you some coffee and brought it across. Or perhaps after all that you could do with a brandy?'

'Coffee will be fine. I'll have something to eat later. Jacob said he'd leave a bite for me.' He looked in the fridge and Leila glimpsed a mountainous stack of sandwiches; great slices of brown bread and thick pink ham. Used to seeing navvy's food, she wasn't too surprised at the size of them, but thought it an understatement to speak of such a plateful as a 'bite'.

She poured coffee for them both and they sat at the table by the side window. It reminded her of the breakfast they'd shared in Hawaii, and she said, 'This is a bit like the morning we met, isn't it?'

'A bit,' he agreed, watching her.

As they drank their coffee in silence she realised once again how very little she knew about him. He was a successful builder and developer, he lived in Coventry, appeared to be unmarried, and was probably more than friendly with Turquoise-Eyes. That was the sum total of her knowledge of him. Why then did she have this crazy feeling of knowing him very well indeed?

'Matt, the woman who called here for you the other day, I think I saw her on Hawaii.'

He regarded her, unperturbed. 'Iris? Yes, she was there when we were. You met her at Cowper's that day, though, surely?'

'Yes. I was introduced to her, but I was so on edge that morning that I soon forgot her name. Is she one of the family?'

He nodded. 'On her mother's side. She's Iris Hamilton, actually, and Rob Cowper's cousin.'

'She's very lovely,' said Leila sincerely. 'Clever as well, I imagine.'

'Yes. Iris is bright,' he agreed non-committally. He picked up a clean shirt and shrugged into it. Leila watched the muscles of his chest expand and contract beneath the taped-up gash.

'Matt, do you want to leave it for now, the stuff about the boating lake? I'm sure you'd like to rest.'

'Rest?' He repeated the word as if it were from an unknown language. 'No, let's get it over with now so that I know exactly what you have in mind.' He went to the desk with her plan and pored over it intently. In the silence Leila thought of his almost total recall of her earth-levels, and decided that by comparison he was making heavy weather of this one.

'The island you suggest, Leila; do you want it to be purely ornamental?'

'Yes, solely for its visual appeal. I thought any obvious access would encourage youngsters to land there and let their boats go floating out of reach and so on. As for the far side of the lake, I see it built up on a slope with shrubs and vegetation right to the water's edge. I hope to plant some semi-mature trees there, as well.'

'Mm. Go on. The same for the island?'

'Rock-based, I thought, then rubble for drainage. Top soil to a good depth for trees and shrubs, and spring bulbs in drifts here and there.'

'We have plenty of hard-core and rubble to get rid of,' he said thoughtfully, 'more than we'll need for levelling off under the tennis courts. All that can be done by us, of course. The actual cleaning and dredging of the water I'd like done by experts.' They discussed the enlarging of the lake and various methods of altering the shape, then he said, 'Come here, Leila,' and dragged forward a chair for her.

'These little sluices to keep the water fresh. You show the inflow ducted from the drains from the playing-fields and also from the rain culverts in the main car-park?'

'That's right. Then the outflow from the lake feeds the stream that goes through the grounds in front of the sports hall and alongside the picnic area. Finally, it goes back into the lake inflow again.'

'Ingenious. But the drainage from the car-park will be tainted with petrol,' he pointed out gently. 'There's bound to be a high petrol content in any such inflow.'

'I know,' she said. 'That's why I've specified the petrol interceptor.' With an effort she kept her voice free of resentment. Did he see her as a novice to neglect provision for the tanks which would filter out the petrol? 'Look.' She leaned across and pointed. 'Here.' Her mouth opened in dismay. 'Oh,' she said weakly. *She* knew where the interceptor was to be installed, but nobody else would. Because she hadn't shown it. Fool! Colour crept up under her delicate skin. 'I'm sorry, Matt. I haven't detailed that, have I? I'd planned it just here.'

'Good. That's where I visualised it as well. Perhaps you should put it in before morning?'

It occurred to her then that this little session had been fixed for her benefit rather than Matt's. Whether or not that was so he'd saved her from looking an incompetent fool in front of the experts. She felt furious with herself. 'Why on earth didn't I notice that I'd missed it out?' she muttered to herself.

'It's a small omission, Leila, and you'd have remembered it soon enough. Off you go now, home.'

She picked up the plan. He'd been incredibly tactful and considerate. 'Thanks, Matt,' she said earnestly, and bestowed on him her radiant smile at full voltage.

He stood up and looked at her, his eyes in shadow. 'You should smile more often,' he said soberly.

'And so should you,' she answered as she left.

It was Friday afternoon, the end of her first working week. Leila sat on a mound of dry earth and looked out across the unpromising stretch of water which was to become the lake. Her vivid imagination covered the opposite bank with a green tracery of trees and shrubs, softened the water-line with rushes and saw how the little island gave serenity to the sparkling water. The meeting that morning had gone well, with the experts accepting her ideas and only questioning one or two minor points. Matt seemed pleased and Peter Larkin had shown a hint of lukewarm approval.

The weekened beckoned, leisurely and inviting. Sam was playing cricket so she and Dee had planned a shopping session. Then on Sunday she was having tea at Ardenfields because it was Agnes's birthday. Over the years she had always had tea with her on that day. She jumped to her feet, ready to forget all about the site until Monday.

Matt waylaid her near the main gate. 'Rob Cowper's been trying to get you on the phone,' he said, 'but you were out on the site somewhere so he rang me.'

'Oh, did he say what he wanted?'

'To invite you to a barbecue at the Cowper place next Saturday evening. It's one of their dos for all those connected with the Foundation. The family are keen on entertaining anybody working on Bequest projects.'

Leila felt a little more enthusiastic. It might not be so bad if Rob's ebullience was subdued by the presence of his family, and he'd hardly try any cave-man tactics with them around. She could do with some social life. 'Where is their place?' she asked.

'It's a Georgian mansion off the beaten track between Warwick and Stratford. Very swish.'

She couldn't help feeling curious. 'Is it Rob's home?'

'Yes. I think he has a flat somewhere in the city, as well. His parents live there and various members of the family. I told him you'd ring him on Monday and that seemed to pacify him.'

'He needed pacifying?' asked Leila drily. 'All right, I'll ring him. As it's a Bequest thing I suppose I'd better go.'

'With me?' he asked. 'I'm going as well.'

'But what about Iris?' she asked curiously. 'Won't you want to pair off with her?'

'No,' he answered calmly. 'Not if I take you.'

Leila's ideas on his relationship with Iris remained unchanged. The sixth sense which could be a curse as well as an asset told her they were lovers. But the idea of having him with her as a bulwark against Rob held distinct appeal.

'I'd love to go with you, Matt. Thanks.'

'We'll fix up about times, etc. next week. Have a good weekend, I expect you're ready for it.'

'I am,' she agreed ruefully. 'What about you? Will you be at home?'

'Yes. I want to go to the office tomorrow and on Sunday I must calculate a tender for a local authority.'

She glanced at his caravan, perplexed. 'But—do you have an office?'

'Of course I do. In Coventry,' he said in amusement. 'Do you think I do all the paperwork in the caravan? No chance. I can only deal with oddments here. It takes a fair-sized staff to look after the firm for me. It's quite complicated, running several projects simultaneously.'

Minutes later she headed the XJS for the motorway

and home, wondering why it hadn't dawned on her that Matt must run a busy office, in addition to overseeing the sites.

She was ready for bed before she realised that a full day had passed without her having had a single remorseful thought about either her father or Lance. Her mind seemed to be filled with Matt Parnell and work, in that order.

'Well, you've put a bit more flesh on your bones,' declared Agnes, after accepting Leila's birthday wishes and her gift of old-fashioned underwear.

Arlene was in London, so they shared a birthday tea with Maisie and Jack in Agnes's sunny sitting room overlooking the orchard. Leila was touched to see her favourite cakes and savouries on the table, and thought that it was more a tea-party for her than a birthday tea for Agnes.

'Maisie, it all looks lovely,' she said warmly. 'You're encouraging me to make a pig of myself.'

As usual, Maisie smiled placidly and said nothing, while Jack, also as usual, ate with concentration. Agnes, however, was intent on giving Leila the third degree about her job. 'You mean to say you're the only woman on the site?' she asked, outraged. 'Well, I do think it seems a bit—forward.'

'Better than seeming backward,' Leila reasoned mildly. 'There were never any women on Dad's sites, Agnes, apart from a cook now and again.'

'How many men work there?' asked Agnes.

'About a hundred. Many hands make light work. Safety in numbers, you know.' A slight curve of the lips indicated that Agnes was amused. She knew Leila liked to tease her about her fondness for quoting proverbs.

'It's not suitable,' she decreed. 'But we must move with the times, I suppose.'

'Enter the twentieth century,' agreed Leila gravely.

'And after all, it *is* Mr Parnell's site.' The housekeeper's double chin became still for a moment as she considered that aspect. 'He isn't the one to let anything happen to you.'

Leila was amused. 'He's obviously made a great impression on you after only one meeting.'

'Two,' said Agnes. 'Two meetings. We had a nice little chat when he was here on Wednesday.'

Leila gaped. 'Here? On Wednesday? Matt Parnell was here?' It was an effort to avoid squeaking. 'What on earth for?'

'To view the house, of course. Didn't he tell you?'

'No,' said Leila thoughtfully. 'He didn't.'

'I think the lady liked it just as much as he did,' said Agnes judiciously.

'Oh.' Leila bent forward to cushion the shock of being struck by a brutal fist right under the ribs. It was half a minute before she realised that nobody had touched her, and that the others were watching her curiously. 'A—a lady you say? Was she dark and beautiful with turquoise eyes?'

'Yes, that's her,' said Agnes.

'But—did they give you the impression that they were looking for a house for them both?' It was odd but she couldn't frame the question more explicitly.

'You mean did they give the impression that they're going to get married? That I couldn't say. After all, your stepmother showed them round. I just chatted to Mr Parnell for a moment while the ladies were in the kitchen.'

'Oh,' said Leila, again, inadequately.

CHAPTER NINE

DRAIN-PIPES, bulldozers and cement mixers were all very well, thought Leila, but they were a bit lacking in aesthetic appeal. The scene outside her window was composed of ugly shapes in brown or grey, and the only splashes of colour came from the garishly painted machinery. She felt starved for the delicacy of leaves and petals, hungry for beauty. Cut flowers were out— Rob's crystal vase was pushed to the back of the cupboard—but she could have some potted plants . . .

With a variegated ivy and a pink pelargonium on her work-bench the next morning she felt so cheered that she decided to bring in some more. Already she felt different on the site because of her sex and her little luxury cabin, so would it really matter if she made herself even more different by having flowering plants cascading past her window, and pots of fuchsias by the door? She decided it wouldn't.

The wooden verandah with its upright supports provided an ideal home for both climbing and hanging plants, and soon it was transformed by bright flowers and greenery. She knew though, that she must restrain herself. 'Enough's enough,' she said aloud as she stood on a chair watering the hanging baskets. 'I will not bring in one more plant.'

'Quite a little bower you've made for yourself,' commented a familiar voice behind her. It was Matt, standing in that deceptively lazy attitude, watching her.

For a moment she thought he was objecting. 'You don't mind, do you?'

'No,' he said easily. 'I can't see the men rushing to follow suit. But I've been wondering what's happened to your dislike of being different.'

It was a good question. She stayed balanced on the chair with the watering can still outstretched while she considered it. Then she jumped down and faced him.

'I've realised that I am different whether I like it or not. I'm happy here on the site, but I do *miss* plants and colour and pretty things to look at. So—I've provided some—that's all.'

He began to answer that, but saw Pete Larkin coming towards them, and waited to see what he wanted. The site agent approached, frowning with concentration on some unknown issue. Then he walked straight past them without so much as a glance in their direction. Leila sighed, exasperated. She had thought she was making some headway with him.

At her side, Matt watched the departing figure thoughtfully. 'Don't let him get you down, Leila,' he warned. 'He's worried about his marriage, or what's left of it. I don't think the men know yet but they've all realised he's not his usual self. He doesn't say much, but he's under a lot of strain.'

She stared after Larkin's broad back, her heart wrenched by sudden pity. He wasn't an easy man to get along with, but hadn't she already sensed a loneliness about him? A need?

'He's worried as hell about his wife and children,' went on Matt, 'and I'm worried as hell about whether he'll keep on top of the job.'

She glanced at him quickly *He* was worried? That calm, decisive manner of his gave no hint of it.

'About tomorrow evening, Leila. Shall I pick you up about eight? It will be an hour's run from Edgbaston to the Cowper place.'

'That'll be fine,' she agreed, 'although it's a long way round for you to come to the flat. How about me driving to Coventry and we'll both go on from there?'

He shook his head reprovingly. 'We both know you don't *need* picking up, Leila; but when I take a girl out I *take* her. Even when it's connected with business. Eight o'clock. I have your address.'

With that he went towards the playing-fields, and a moment later she heard the helicopter start up. She stood there, still clutching the watering-can. He hadn't yet said one word about visiting Ardenfields with Iris Hamilton, and she certainly didn't feel like asking him

about it. Were he and Iris engaged? Were they looking
for their future home?

Engaged or not, he was aiming to take her, Leila, to
the Cowper barbecue. He'd just made clear, though,
that he saw it as an outing connected with business . . .
With an impatient shrug, Leila went inside and started
work again. She was leaving early to keep her
appointment with the lawyer, Mr Dobbs.

Leila climbed Bennetts Hill and made for the car-park.
She'd been with Mr Dobbs almost an hour, during
which she'd learned a lot and said very little.

Because she felt guilty about his fruitless attempts to
contact her, she'd let him drone on uninterrupted,
prepared for a lecture on her extravagance during her
time with Lance. Eventually it became clear that far
from remonstrating with her about how much she'd
spent he was gently congratulating her upon her thrift!

She was baffled. 'Mr Dobbs, will you please tell me
what I'm worth? In total. The lump sum from the
takeover, the realising of the annuity, the stocks and
securities, everything.'

Mr Dobbs stretched his long neck with some
satisfaction. 'I contacted your accountant several days
ago, anticipating such a question. As at 4 p.m.
yesterday, a total of four hundred and sixty-nine
thousand, seven hundred and fifty-one pounds. That is,
of course, excluding the amount in your cheque account
and your No 2 deposit account.'

Leila sat there and tried to look intelligent. 'It's a lot
more than I anticipated,' she said at last, limply.

'Your father was a very meticulous man.' Mr Dobbs
made the statement sound like the highest accolade he
could offer. Once again Leila was caught by a mental
picture of her father working on the draft of his will.
She felt horribly close to tears as Mr Dobbs went into
more detail about her investments.

'Yes,' she agreed, ten minutes later, 'yes, go ahead
and invest the capital as you think fit. And you're quite
certain that Mr and Mrs Binns and Agnes MacLean are
well-provided for?'

Reassured on that point she prepared to leave. 'Goodbye, Mr Dobbs. Please ensure that you are suitably reimbursed for your efforts.'

Leila strode through the busy streets, torn between tears at the evidence of her father's concern and laughter at her 'ensure' and 'reimbursed'. The legal jargon had got to her, it seemed. But almost half a million! And no provisos about her future ... no mention of her marrying ... no instructions about how she was to handle the money ... All at once, as clearly as if he'd spoken at her side, she knew that her father was saying, through his will, 'It's your life—make something of it—it's up to you.'

If she wished, she could buy Ardenfields from Arlene. If she'd been in England at the time of the takeover maybe she could have bought Garlands and run it herself. If she felt capable, she could buy her own small building and developing company ... If ... if ... if ...

Deep in thought, she made her way through the busy streets, but within minutes her mind was back on the problem of altering the shrubbery around the main building.

The site was deserted except for Charlie, but Leila wanted to finish revising her plans. She would enjoy her weekend all the more if the whole sequence was finished and up on the walls as Matt had requested.

She needed one last look at the foundations of the main building, where, at Martin Deeds' insistence, she was altering her original plan of raised beds of shrubs in the angle of the walls.

She clambered across the trenches and mounds of earth, feeling a little guilty. Pete Larkin had warned her about being on the site alone in case she had an accident, so she moved with care to where two angles formed the sides of the entrance.

Moments later she still stood there, her measure in her hand. Surely the two sides should be exact right angles? And hadn't she checked it as 0.4 of a metre above ground level and the head of the wheelchair ramp at exactly one metre?

She stood there, biting uncertainly on her lower lip.
They couldn't have done it wrong. Pete Larkin
supervised all bricklaying measurements as he must
surely have supervised the footings, and—Pete Larkin!
She remembered his expression that morning.
Withdrawn, remote, intent on some unknown issue.
No—she was mad. Who was she to query the work of a
civil engineer and a gang of qualified bricklayers?

But suppose she was right and there *had* been a
botch-up? She couldn't let the men carry on. On
impulse she went and asked Charlie for his key to
Matt's caravan. 'It's just to check on the big blow-up of
the architect's plan,' she explained. 'I don't think Mr
Parnell would mind——'

'No,' agreed Charlie placidly. 'He wouldn't. He told
me you can have the run of everything.'

'Oh. That's—that's nice,' she said faintly, and
unlocked the door. Her nose twitched. It smelled of
Matt. Clean, unscented, vaguely antiseptic. She smiled.
It was the antiseptic that reminded her of him. He'd
told her his chest was healing well. It was some
consolation for the harrowing session cleaning that
gash.

Carefully she examined the blow-up. She saw at once
that she was right, but she'd have to check on Larkin's
copy as well. As she turned to leave she noticed
something on Matt's desk by the window. It was an old
issue of a surfing magazine, one she remembered well.
The cover showed Lance, lean and golden, riding the
towering surf on one of the Thai beaches. Inside that
issue, she knew, was an interview with him, and
photographs, one of which showed her and Lance
laughing together over a cook-out on the beach. Why
had Matt got it? *How* had he got it? By accident? She
shook her head, baffled, and hurried to ask Charlie for
the other key.

Both sets of plans tallied with hers. She pictured
Martin Deeds' reaction if he should visit the site
unexpectedly. And should she tell Pete Larkin or Matt?
She decided to tackle the site agent direct, perhaps she'd
manage a private word with him at the barbecue.

*   *   *

Leila sat at Matt's side as they sped along the Warwick road. He was driving a four-year-old Ford estate with a few dents and scratches on the wing and a smell of new timber inside it. She was surprised, having half-expected him to arrive in the sort of car a wealthy businessman would drive for pleasure. His money went into the company, apparently. No Aston-Martin for him.

He had rung the doorbell just as she fastened her high-heeled sandals. She was wearing a leaf-green silk jump-suit with bootlace straps, bought on her shopping spree with Dee, and for once had spent time on her appearance; reflecting that apart from lunch at the Albany with Rob, this was her first outing with a man since Matt had taken her to the coral island.

'Leila,' he said. No 'Hello' or 'Hi' or 'Am I too early?' Just 'Leila.' For a moment he hesitated before crossing the threshold, his clear eyes observing her slender form in the leaf-green silk, noting the satin-smooth shoulders and the hair falling in its deep, honey-gold waves. As always, she wore the heavy gold chain that her father had bought her.

His devastating smile flashed out, and at the sight of it she felt her heart lift as surely as if a set of strings and pulleys had gone into action inside her chest. 'You look very beautiful,' he said quietly, and followed her inside.

He was wearing cream slacks and a copper-coloured shirt, and looked expensively casual. She was so used to seeing him in working clothes she was fascinated, just as she'd been that morning when he returned to the site in evening clothes.

He accepted a vodka with lots of ice and looked at the split-level room with a professional eye. 'A good conversion,' he commented. 'Will you show me round?'

She led the way up the spiral staircase and saw him smile again when he saw the Victorian bath with its fat pink roses. 'Roses, roses all the way,' he said musingly. 'A rose by any other name ... J.T. Rose ... Do you know what I call you?'

Startled, she looked up at him. What was coming now?

'Capability Rose,' he said gently. 'It suits you, you know. The feminine, up-to-the-minute-version of Capability Brown himself.'

She passed it off with a chuckle, but secretly she was touched. It was a terrific compliment. They went back downstairs and Matt crossed to her easel by the rear window. A big painting was there, half-completed, her mental vision of what the site would look like when it was finished and all the trees and plants were established. She liked doing water-colours, and had often used the medium to advantage in her degree work.

He examined it closely. 'You have a very clear idea of what all your hard work will lead to, don't you? Is this destined to embellish your office the same as your plants and baskets?'

She smiled. 'Yes. A foretaste of what's to come when it's all done.'

Those few minutes of easy companionship had started the evening off well, she thought, stealing a look at the no-nonsense profile at her side. They left the main road and entered a network of country lanes. It was still daylight but the shadows were lengthening over the lush green fields, with the sun picking out an occasional half-timbered cottage. Leila felt a warm glow of contentment. She was with a man whose company she enjoyed, driving on a warm summer evening through her home county. She loved the Warwickshire countryside, the rich earth, the gently sloping hills, and the ancient villages with their half-timbered houses.

'Nearly there,' murmured Matt, driving alongside a high wall and then slowing for a lodge-gate. A burly man with an Alsatian dog at his side examined the car's occupants and waved them on, recognising Matt. It was Leila's first reminder that they were entering millionaire territory. A mile further on they passed through a second security check and soon the house came into view.

It was very large, very white and very beautiful. On rising ground, with open country all around and the pink-tinged Avon curving lazily across distant fields under a reddening sky. Leila picked up the gold leather gilet she'd bought in Australia, a last-minute addition to her outfit when she realised belatedly that barbecues were held out of doors, even in England.

A uniformed maid took them both to the rear of the house, where a big sitting room was open to a huge terrace bright with lanterns. A crowd of people were there, some of them at a long buffet table, others collecting steaks from the glowing grills.

Matt was still by her side as they stepped outside, and immediately Rob bounded forward. He was wearing a pink shirt and black Ralph Lauren cords tucked into cowboy boots. His hair was already defying control and stood out in wild disorder all over his head. Leila found herself liking him again. She thought he resembled a large ten-year-old playing at cowboys; he only needed toy six-shooters and a plastic gun-belt.

The look in his eyes was hardly that of a ten-year-old, though, as he took in her appearance. 'Great to see you, Leila. You look terrific.' His warm hand on her wrist said what the welcoming words left out. It said he was prepared to forget their last meeting and told her that the restrictions she'd imposed at the site didn't apply in his own home. As if just noticing Matt, he said, 'Oh, hi there, Matt. Let me get you both a drink.'

He dragged her off on a tour of introductions, one hand firmly clamped on the soft flesh above her elbow, while Matt stood alone by the grills, waiting. She soon found that the Cowper family were numerous, pleasant and without exception knowledgeable about the work of the Foundation. She met Rob's parents; pleasant, middle-aged people with no evidence of extreme wealth about them apart from their clothes and the relaxed way in which they watched their guests enjoying hospitality which had cost a small fortune. The name Hamilton registered, and Leila found herself facing an older version of Iris—her mother, plump but still lovely with Iris's exceptional eyes set in the faintest network of wrinkles.

A maid came to Rob asking him to take a phone call from New York, and as soon as he'd gone Leila made her way back to Matt. 'I seem to have met a hundred Cowpers in ten minutes,' she said ruefully. 'Ten a minute, that's too many. Let's wander away while Rob's on the phone.'

Matt looked at her consideringly. 'He doesn't seem to be leaving you alone,' he said coolly.

'Leaving me alone? Oh, you mean like I told him to at the site? No, it doesn't look as if he got the message, or if he did he's decided to forget it. Somehow he doesn't seem quite so objectionable here against his own background.'

'No?' He looked round, his gaze travelling slowly over the crowded terraces, the sumptuous buffet, the chefs behind their glowing grills. 'But then, it's a pretty impressive background, isn't it?'

She smiled and nodded. 'It certainly is, it's lovely. I've never been in such a magnificent house in my life.' Then the implication of his remark hit her. Was he saying that she found Rob more attractive now that she'd seen material evidence of the Cowper fortunes— seen the country estate in all its splendour? Her enormous eyes sought Matt's for confirmation. She got it. His were cold as winter sea under a leaden sky.

Sudden fury made her look away. How *could* he imply that she was influenced by the Cowper trappings? Some perverse impulse came to her then, overriding her desire to explain to him in words of one syllable that Rob's money meant nothing to her, that, in fact, she could probably match his wealth with her own. If Matt judged her to be a gold-digger then she'd give him something to confirm the idea. She took a long slow drink of her wine, twirled the glass in her fingers and said, 'Well, a set-up like this could make a girl look favourably on a chimpanzee, couldn't it?'

Grimly pleased, she saw amazement register on the tough, battered features; the high-bridged nose was lifted even higher, the shapely lips pressed more tightly together. He stared fixedly across the wide expanse of terrace to where drummers and a limbo dancer were taking their places, and remained silent.

Leila felt shattered. More—she felt humiliated. She

must have been insane to sit next to him in the car and
imagine that she was going to enjoy the evening. She
turned to leave his side when a well-known voice halted
her. 'Matt! I didn't know you'd be here!' It was Arlene,
closely followed by Bernard.

Astounded, Leila watched her stepmother, fairy-doll
pretty in tight blue pants and a white sparkly top, plant
an enthusiastic kiss on Matt's mouth. Her warm smile
cooled rapidly when she saw who was next to him.
'Leila! What are you doing here?'

'I was invited, Arlene, because I work for the Cowper
Foundation. I didn't realise you and Matt knew each
other?'

'Of course we do.' Arlene linked one hand through
his arm and the other through Bernard's. 'Bern is
accountant for one of the Cowper holdings now, that's
why we're here. But Matt is an old friend, aren't you,
Matt?'

'You could say that,' agreed Matt pleasantly. 'Arlene
and I saw a lot of each other at the time of the
takeover, Leila.'

Of course. She should have thought of that. Bernard
leaned towards her, his arm still in Arlene's grasp. 'How
are things with you, Leila?'

She looked at him. The inevitable medallion swung
against his chest and the floral shirt was open to the
waist. The amorous accountant. Bernard was kind
enough in his way though, and just now his heavy
features were full of concern.

For the first time in years she didn't proffer her cheek
for a kiss on meeting him. Those days were over. 'I'm
well, Bernard, thanks. Working at last. For Cowper, on
one of Matt's sites. Congratulations on your new
position with them; are you——'

'Let's get a table,' interrupted Arlene, 'the three of us,
there, under the trees. Oh—Leila, aren't you with
anyone?'

'I *was* with Matt,' she answered quietly, 'but there's
someone I know over there, I think. I'll see you all
later.' Without a backward glance she threaded her way
through the crowd.

The elegant cloakroom was deserted. She ran her hands under the cold tap and dried them on a linen towel embroidered with a black 'C'. She twisted it tightly before examining it as if it was vitally important. Like the rest of the Cowper possessions it showed taste; understated but confident.

She sat in front of a mirror and stared dully at her reflection. That waxy look was on her cheeks. The colour left her face in a hurry whenever she was upset. And she was upset now by two separate incidents in the course of two minutes. First by what Matt had said and then by Arlene's attitude. Why did it trouble her that Arlene didn't like her? She knew her stepmother to be shallow and full of self-interest, so why worry about it?

She leaned back in the chair, considering the question. Perhaps it was because Arlene was her step*mother*. The only mother she'd known since she was a little girl ... the woman her father had married ... the woman he'd—been fond of. She couldn't form the thought—'the woman he'd loved'.

For ten minutes she sat there, cold in spite of the warm evening. The noise of the party was increasing now that the drummers had started. Why had she come here? Why hadn't she stayed at home and painted more of her landscape? All at once that solitary occupation seemed safe and secure and infinitely to be treasured.

Two middle-aged women bustled in, talking non-stop. Leila took out her comb and tidied her hair, then renewed her lipstick. She smiled at them both and went back to the party, outwardly composed and self-assured.

The first person she saw outside was Pete Larkin drinking at the bar. Her heart sank. She'd forgotten all about the problems of the foundations. But he'd seen her and gave a nod and a slight smile in her direction. 'Get it over with,' she thought. 'The evening's a shambles already, it can't deteriorate much more.' He appeared gratified when she joined him. Something in his attempt at nonchalance told her that he wasn't used to being on his own at affairs of this sort. 'Hello, Mr Larkin, have you been here long?'

'No,' he said shortly. 'I've just arrived. You came with Matt, I believe?'

'Yes. I'd like a word with you if it's convenient?'

'Why not? Business before pleasure. A drink?'

'Not now, thanks.' They found seats on a stone bench nearby, but when faced by the pale hard eyes Leila felt at a loss. How did one tell a civil engineer that he was botching up the job?

She took a deep breath. 'Mr Larkin. I know this isn't my business and I'm probably wrong anyway, but yesterday I had to look at the foundations of the main building to check my alterations to the shrubbery beds I'd planned by the front entrance.'

He was looking at her blankly. 'Yes?'

'Well, as I say, it's none of my business but I couldn't help noticing that the line of the footings isn't like that of the plan, and the height of the ramp seems a bit funny . . .'

'A bit funny?' he repeated. 'Don't you think it's a bit funny that nobody else has noticed anything wrong?'

'Of course I do. But I checked Matt's plan and then the one in your office, just in case yours had been altered and not Matt's. Then this morning I wondered if perhaps you'd got mixed up between the main entrance and the one at the rear of the swimming complex. They're a bit alike.'

'Why should I do that?' He sounded genuinely puzzled.

'Because—because you've got a lot on your mind—I mean——' Her voice trailed off.

Without a word he left her and went back to the bar. He came back with another whisky. 'It's common talk then?' he asked tightly. 'Larkin can't keep his wife, eh?'

'No, not common talk,' she protested gently. 'Matt told me in confidence that you were having a little trouble with your marriage.' This was worse than she'd anticipated.

'A little trouble!' he echoed derisively. 'And what does Matt say, in confidence, about your ideas on the footings? I'm sure he's been over there to see them for himself. How come he hasn't tackled me yet?'

'Because I haven't told him,' she said.

Her heart twisted in sympathy at the conflict of emotions on his face. Surprise, embarrassment, humiliation. This was a self-sufficient man, and it was coming hard having a girl he despised watching over his interests.

'Why haven't you? He's the boss.'

'You're in charge of the brickies, aren't you? I thought it might be—better if I asked you first, that's all.'

At that he turned his full attention on her. She felt that for the first time he saw her as a person rather than a faceless, unwelcome amateur on the job. He stared at her in silence, gnawing his lower lip as if lost for words.

Over his shoulder she saw yet another person she would be glad to avoid. 'Here's Martin Deeds coming our way,' she said hurriedly. 'I'll leave you together.' She walked away, nodding casually to the architect and his bird-like little wife. Deeds turned his carroty head away, pretending he hadn't seen her.

'It's lovely to be so popular,' she told herself bitterly. 'Why on earth have I come?'

CHAPTER TEN

LEILA found that she was still popular with one person, however. Rob grabbed her shoulders from behind and whirled her round. 'So there you are! I've been looking everywhere. Parnell's sandwiched between Iris and some dizzy blonde and hadn't a clue where you'd gone, and that Larkin guy who's glued to the bar said he didn't know either.'

'I've just been talking to him. Did you take your call from the States?'

He nodded. 'It was our New York lawyer. It's four o'clock in the afternoon their time and he's still in the office! I ask you! Come on, they're playing an old-fashioned smoochy. Let's dance.'

Making no attempt to look for Matt she let herself be led towards a specially laid dance floor on the lower terrace. The band was playing softly, a full moon hung over the trees and the great white house glowed warmly behind them, every window alight. She began to feel better, her love of beauty responding to the sheer magic of the scene. 'Even the weather behaves itself for the Cowpers,' she teased.

'Moonlight to order,' he agreed, laughing delightedly.

'And there aren't even any gnats or mosquitos around.'

'Oh, we always get rid of those in advance,' he said, quite as if the Cowpers ordered the whole of the Midlands to be sprayed. 'We don't want this lovely skin getting bitten, do we?' He ran exploratory fingers across her bare shoulders, grinning, then took her in his arms to dance. She found it wasn't unpleasant. He held her tight and rested his head against hers, but he kept his hands under control. She sensed the restless, pent-up energy in him, and thought that he would never be a peaceful companion in a thousand years.

He whirled her round madly when the music finished

120

as if eager for action again, and she laughed up at him. It wasn't possible to be unmoved by Rob. One could either like him or detest him, but to ignore him would be impossible. At that moment she liked him.

'Let's go for some steaks,' he said, holding her hand.

She saw Matt, then, leaving the floor with Iris. The dark-haired girl looked stunning in a casually draped grey dress which covered her up to the neck both back and front, but was open at the sides almost down to the hips, giving glimpses of taut, suntanned breasts. Her legs were bare and she wore flat pink sandals. She looked carelessly elegant and very sexy, and Leila caught sight of Matt's brown, hairy hand laid behind her waist.

Moments later Iris herself appeared next to her at the buffet, loading a plate with salad and lobster. 'Hello, it's Leila, isn't it? Matt's been telling me about your work at the site. I'm Iris Hamilton, I think we met at the Foundation's rooms some weeks ago.'

Leila looked into the dazzling aquamarine eyes. She didn't know why she was so surprised to find herself liking the other woman.

'Matt's over there claiming a table,' said Iris. 'I've told Rob to bring you over.' She moved gracefully away on a drift of perfume just as Rob leapt to Leila's side.

'Lord! Iris is such a bossy devil,' he said disgustedly. 'Do you really want to go and eat with them? I've got a secluded little summer-house for two laid on, with masses of cushions and champagne already on ice.'

Leila stared at him, frosty-eyed. She didn't in the least want to join Iris and Matt but it looked like being the best of two unpleasant alternatives. Cushions for two in a summer-house? No chance.

'All right, all right!' He put up a hand. 'Spare me another icy blast from those big brown eyes.' He tried without success to conceal his pique. 'We'll join Iris and her bricklayer. He did bring you after all.' They walked down the steps together. 'Two of the old guys from the Bequest committee want to talk to you after we've eaten,' he added, and sent a passing waiter in search of champagne.

Iris and Matt were waiting for them at one of the tables on the lawn. Her stepmother and Bernard were nowhere in sight, for which Leila was thankful. If she'd been in a happier frame of mind she might have enjoyed that moonlit meal; hot juicy steaks, exotic salads, strawberries and cream and champagne, but she had no appetite. She felt on the verge of some disturbing discovery and her mind forged ahead, searching for clues as to what it could be. 'Iris and her bricklayer' Rob had said, and now she found herself studying Matt's profile outlined against the lanterns and fairy lights. Not once did he turn his head in her direction. She might as well have been invisible.

It was comforting to have Rob so attentive, eager to grant her smallest wish; and Iris too was charming, showing genuine interest in her work and asking intelligent questions about it. Leila chatted easily to her and Rob but it was as if a separate compartment of her mind was making its own valuations, coming to its own conclusions.

Ever since the day when Iris called for Matt at the site, Leila had wondered how they felt about each other. Her interest in their relationship had mounted when Agnes revealed that they had visited Ardenfields together. Now, her curiosity was satisfied, at least in part. Iris was a sophisticated woman, highly intelligent and self-disciplined, but she couldn't conceal that she was in love with Matt. There was no open display of it, of course, only those magnificent eyes betrayed her, watching his every move, constantly searching for his glance, even while she talked brightly to Rob and Leila.

Suddenly cold, Leila found her gold gilet and put it on. She leaned towards Iris. 'I believe you visited my old home recently, Iris. Ardenfields. Are you and Matt looking for a property in that particular area?'

'Not that specific area, no. But we *are* looking.' Iris smiled serenely across the table, while Leila fought the urge to press her fist tightly against her chest. It hurt.

Iris went on, 'Matt's being an angel and vetting anything reasonable that comes up. It's a lovely house, Leila.'

'Thank you. My father built it when I was ten.' Rob leaned forward and spoke, but Leila missed hearing what he said. Surely that was an odd remark from Iris? 'Matt's being an angel and vetting anything.' Of course he'd be vetting it if he was going to buy it . . .

She knew that he had turned his head at last and was watching her and Iris with close attention. 'Dad thinks something not so far out would be better,' went on Iris. 'He hates driving into the city.'

'Your *father*?' asked Leila. 'But surely——'

'It's my parents who want a house,' said Iris, laughing. 'Not Matt and me! For years they've had a wing of the family place, here, but recently Dad's been hankering for a house of their own.'

Leila ate her strawberries and said no more. She knew Matt's eyes had been on her during that little exchange. Rob poured her more champagne and she wondered if she felt light-hearted or light-headed—or both.

There was a roll of drums and the next entertainer came out on the lower terrace. It was a fire-eater. They had a good view and so stayed at the table, while the man went through his amazing performance.

And there, under the lamplit trees, with a full moon hanging in the heavens and applause rippling through the crowd, Leila knew what that disturbing discovery had turned out to be, and it wasn't that Iris was in love with Matt, significant though that was.

She remembered sitting up in bed in Hawaii, watching a full moon there and resolving to return early to England rather than get involved with Matt. Now, ten weeks later, she was in England under another full moon and she was more involved with him than ever. She loved him. The fact that he wasn't going to marry Iris was the best news she'd ever heard.

The crowd shouted their approval and the drums rolled. Rob and Iris made teasing remarks to each other, the band started to play, but Leila sat silently, reviewing her own feelings and reactions to Matt, from the time she ran into the lagoon on Hawaii to the hurt she'd felt earlier that evening, when he implied that she was after Rob's money. That had been bad but it was as nothing to the searing knife-thrust of pain she'd felt when she believed that he and Iris had inspected Ardenfields as a future home.

She sighed deeply. So much for her resolve not to get involved. Involvement with Lance had brought her brief joy, then untold pain and misery. Nothing on God's earth would make her suffer that again.

It was two in the morning and the party had been indoors since before midnight. Some people were leaving, and Leila was ready, more than ready, to go home. It had been a vile evening. Arlene and Bernard were still there; her stepmother a little bit tight now, and Bernard was trying to quieten her. Pete Larkin had stayed by the bar, drinking, and Martin Deeds had joined uninvited in her discussion with the two elderly members of the Bequest Committee and had succeeded in making her look amateurish and ineffectual.

Then there was Rob. The attentiveness which had at first been a comfort quickly became a nuisance. She had seen that he didn't relish being near her for several hours without more physical contact than that of the dance floor, and the last straw had been his attempt to take her 'for a stroll down to the lake'.

Minutes later he led her to a deep alcove near the band and said, as if making a supremely generous offer, 'Look, Leila, I like you a lot but I want you to know that I'm prepared to wait a bit longer. I found out about your boyfriend dying and I can see you're still upset about it—so I've decided to give you a few more weeks to get over it and then we'll go places together.'

It was an incredibly irritating little speech, but it was late, and she was tired, and what was more she thought his dark eyes held a hint of pleading. Perhaps he felt more for her than she'd imagined? He waited for her answer and she saw colour creep up under his cheekbones. It was something that happened from time to time with Rob, a slight flush of the cheeks which perhaps indicated that he was less confident than he seemed. She smiled gently, unwilling to hurt him.

'Thanks, Rob. That's very—very thoughtful of you.' And in a way it was. Patience would be unknown to Rob Cowper, she thought. He would get tired of waiting, and then perhaps he would leave her alone.

Iris and Matt joined them. 'Look, Leila,' said Iris, 'it's late and you both have a long drive home. Why don't you and Matt stay the night? We're having a quiet day by the pool tomorrow. You could borrow swimming gear and anything you might need for the night. What do you say?'

Leila's heart sank. Her one desire was to get out of the place fast. She looked at Matt to see his reaction, her eyes enormous, and, as always, faintly shadowed. For a few seconds he studied her face, then said, 'I'm afraid I can't possibly, Iris. I have masses of work to do. But if Leila wants to stay——'

'No,' she said quickly. 'Thanks, Iris, but I have something planned for tomorrow. Perhaps another time. I don't want to rush you, Matt, but I'm rather tired——'

'We'll go now,' he agreed. They said their farewells to the senior Cowpers and then to Iris and Rob, who stood side by side, each looking elaborately unconcerned, before going back indoors as Leila and Matt went to the car. There was no moonlight now. Clouds were banking overhead and a small damp wind was blowing.

They both stopped simultaneously. 'Matt, what about Pete Larkin? He isn't fit to drive.'

'I know,' he agreed. 'We can't leave him here. He'll feel like hell in the morning if the Cowpers have to put him to bed.'

'Can we take him with us?'

He looked down at her. 'His car's here. He'll need it for work on Monday.'

'I'll drive him back in it,' she volunteered. 'He lives nearer to my place than yours.'

Matt glared at her impatiently. 'Do you really imagine I'd let you drive to Solihull with a drunk at your side? The Cowpers would send his car over tomorrow, I'm sure of that, but I'd rather not put them to the trouble, Pete would feel bad about it. I'll take him with me if you'll follow behind, in his car. That way he'll have it at home and I can take you back from Solihull.'

He made short work of getting Pete outside. The older man was confused and deep in drunken melancholy, but he let himself be bundled into the car. Matt handed her the keys of Pete's Vauxhall. 'You're sure you'll be all right?' For a moment he looked uncertain, then he told her how to find Pete's house in case they became separated, and they set off.

Driving right behind him, she didn't know whether she was relieved or disappointed to be on her own. She and Matt hadn't spoken a dozen words to each other since their unpleasant exchange soon after arriving, and she'd been dreading the drive back.

As the two cars sped along the quiet roads it came to her that it wasn't at all like Matt to be so unreasonable, to make snap judgments such as the one that had angered her. If it was so out of character, though, why hadn't he spoken to her since? Why hadn't he danced with her?

She looked back on the times he'd actually touched her. They were few, very few. A hand under the elbow, a casual hand-clasp on the coral island, that brief grateful squeeze of her hand after she'd dealt with the gash on his chest ... The most intimate physical contact they'd shared had been at the moment they first met, when his firm grip around her ribs had lifted her from the water; the brisk towelling, the way he had tossed aside her sodden muu-muu ... It seemed light-years since then, an event at another time, in another world. She smiled sadly. Hawaii *was* a long way from the Warwick road and Solihull.

But one thing was clear. He had never, never once touched her as a man touches a woman he finds desirable. There was only one conclusion to be drawn from that. She kept her eyes on the road and closed her mind to everything else.

At last Matt stopped on the drive of a small modern house in a cul-de-sac in Solihull. Pete was fast asleep in the lax, uncoordinated way of the drunk, and remained limp when Matt dragged him from the car and slung him over one shoulder, while Leila unlocked the front door of the empty house. 'I'll put him to bed,' said Matt, and went up the stairs.

Leila went out and replaced Matt's car on the drive with Pete's, then went back and hovered in the hall. Apparently, Pete still lived in the family home. She saw that the hall carpet needed vacuuming and that newspapers were tossed aside behind the door. An air of hopelessness, of despair, pervaded the house. Poor Pete. What had happened to make his wife leave him? Another man? Money troubles?

Matt came down. 'He'll be all right,' he said briefly. 'I've undressed him. Let's go.' They left the keys indoors and locked up, then headed for Edgbaston. It was almost three-thirty.

Leila felt exhausted. The drive home in a strange car had drained her last reserves of vitality. She sank deep into the passenger seat and felt perilously close to tears. Observant as ever, Matt looked sideways at her. 'What is it?' he asked abruptly.

'I'm just a bit tired,' she said. 'And that house! It's so sad, so empty and neglected. How long have they been separated, do you know?'

'About six weeks. Don't think about it now, Leila, you can't do anything.'

The car sped on through quiet roads, the headlights sparkling on fine rain. 'Have you been married, Matt?' It was the last thing she intended saying, and the question fell into the silence like a stone into a quiet pool.

He didn't answer right away, but at last he said, 'You don't know much about me, do you, Leila?'

'I don't know anything,' she admitted, 'except that you own a big building firm and live somewhere in Coventry.' It wasn't her intention to sound so forlorn, so lifeless.

He picked up speed. 'Let's get you home,' he said briskly, 'you're exhausted. I gather you haven't enjoyed the evening.'

'It was ghastly,' she said emptily. 'I can't remember when I enjoyed an evening less.' She stared at the windscreen and watched the rhythmic swish of the wipers. To her horror she felt the sting of tears, and furtively wiped her cheeks with her fingers. He knew she was crying. She saw the sideways flicker of his eyes, felt the car slow down.

Then he picked up speed again and said in a calm, conversational tone, 'Well, I'd better fill in a few details for you, hadn't I? I live just outside Coventry in a thatched cottage that's very different from the stuff I build. My mother lives there with me, and my brothers and sisters are all married. I'm the only one still single. I was on the brink of marriage once, but my bride-to-be changed her mind the day before the wedding. So—in answer to your question—no, I've never been married.'

If it hadn't seemed so unlikely she would have thought he'd told her that deliberately to jerk her out of the misery which lay on her like lead.

'Changed her mind?' she repeated hoarsely. Some girl had left him almost at the altar!

'It's a long time ago,' he said. 'I was twenty-three. She was a typist in the office of the building firm where I worked. She left me for a young executive type.'

Leila ran her tongue over lips that suddenly felt dry. 'A young executive type?' She was repeating everything he said, for crying out loud. 'But—surely you were a young executive type as well?'

'No, I wasn't,' he said simply. 'Not then. I was a bricklayer, only one step up from hod-carrying—a job that's all brawn rather than brain. We'd put a deposit on a little terraced house and that was the limit of my ambitions. To live with Jenny in that house.'

He spoke easily, without bitterness, but in her overwrought state she imagined she heard the echo of past heartbreak in the deep, even tones. 'Oh, how could she? How could she do it?' she muttered.

'I don't think she found it easy,' he said, 'because she knew how I loved her. But she was honest—she didn't fancy being married to a building-site brickie without a penny to his name.'

Leila's ideas were being turned upside down. She'd always thought that Matt had entered the business via a degree or at the very least a NNC. 'What happened then?' she asked, not at all sure now that she wanted to hear it.

'Being jilted almost at the altar changed my life, that's what happened. I decided to climb the ladder, and not as a hod-carrier. Within three years I was building for myself. Two more years and I was a local authority contract.'

'And the girl—Jenny? Was she happy with her young executive type?'

'I think so,' he said slowly. 'I've seen her several times—from a distance, and I met her in the Bull Ring a few months ago. She's plump and pretty and the mother of three girls. Come on, here we are.' They were back at the flat.

He came round and opened her door. She got out and looked up at him. The rain hissed down through the trees and there was a smell of wet earth and roses. She found herself whispering so as not to disturb the ground floor tenants. 'Matt—it's almost morning. Come on up—you can have the spare bedroom.'

He shook his head, and she saw the upwards lift of his mouth. 'You're pretty tired.'

'You can leave as soon as I've given you breakfast if you have work to do. It must be almost four o'clock now. Do stay.' She shivered suddenly. Her arms were wet and the silk trousers were clinging damply to her legs. All she knew was that she mustn't let him go until they were back on the old footing.

He nodded, and together they crept up the stairs to the top floor. She searched for her key and thought: 'This isn't the way to avoid getting involved, Leila Garland.' Then they were inside and she said the first thing that entered her head. 'Let's have a cup of tea!' She switched on the lamps and went to put the kettle on, while Matt prowled restlessly around the room.

They drank mugs of tea while Leila cudgelled her weary wits as to what she wanted to say to him, and Matt remained silent, directing his gaze anywhere but at her face. He was a reasonable man, she thought, kind, considerate. She must tell him—what, exactly?

In the end it was he who broke the silence. 'I'm afraid I upset you very much by what I said at the barbecue about Rob and his background.'

'Yes,' she admitted quietly. This was getting down to it. 'To be fair, though, you didn't actually *say* anything, you implied it. I reacted as I did—that stuff about looking favourably on a chimpanzee—because I was annoyed.'

'And because what I'd implied wasn't true?'

'Of *course* it wasn't true,' she said shortly. 'Rob Cowper is a—an overpowering sort of person. He doesn't like to take no for an answer. I don't think he's even heard the word all that often, and if you must know I think he likes me simply because I haven't thrown myself into his arms.'

It seemed to her that he still looked sceptical. Sudden fury made her forget all about her anxiety to be on friendly terms again. 'I—am—not—remotely—interested—in—Rob—Cowper's—money,' she said slowly and distinctly. 'The fact that you were jilted by a money-grabber doesn't mean that all other women are the same, you know!'

She watched the dark-lashed eyelids come down, shutter-like, over the revealing eyes. 'Clearly put,' he said evenly.

Things were moving rapidly from bad to worse. This was the man who had seen her close to tears and had immediately told her that the girl he'd loved had left him the day before the wedding. It was a story that wouldn't come easily to any man and all she could do in return was to make cheap remarks about it. Her jaws ached, and automatically she ran her hands up and down her cheeks. If she thought she was wrong, Leila didn't mind admitting it.

'I'm sorry, Matt. That was a rotten thing to say. I apologise.'

'Forget it,' he said. 'You're tired, and so am I.'

She went up the staircase, slipped a pillowcase on a spare pillow and twitched the duvet into place on the spare bed, which she kept made up. Then she went back down. 'I've made up the bed, Matt. Give me five minutes in the bathroom and then it's all yours.'

'Good night, Leila,' he said.

'Good night, Matt.'

Halfway up the spiral stairs she stopped, the leaf-green silk wafting damply against her legs. 'I'm truly sorry about Jenny,' she said, looking down at him. 'Did you love her very much?'

'Yes,' he said. 'I loved her very much.'

A voice was screaming hysterically. The surf was roaring, the spume flying landwards from the breakers. Lance was in there, being flung over and over like a piece of driftwood. Nobody else could see him, and Rob Cowper barred her way, arms outstretched, shouting, 'I'll wait. I don't mind waiting.' She couldn't get out to Lance. The water was thigh deep and it was pulling at her. Nobody could hear him calling. The wet blond hair was plastered to his skull and he was being turned over, spun around, broken, mangled. She opened her mouth to call for help but someone was holding her by the shoulders, silencing her. She tried again, she must get help—

'Leila! God in Heaven, Leila! It's all right. It's all right. You're having a nightmare.' The screaming stopped and she heard someone sobbing, gasping. It was her! She was in her own bed. She was the one who'd been screaming. As always, the relief was overpowering. Her eyes streamed with tears and she was bathed in sweat. Tears and sweat, the end products of all her nightmares, running between her breasts and wetting her nightgown.

She shuddered, half her mind still in the undertow on Johanna beach. Gentle arms lifted her from the wet pillow. Someone wiped her eyes with tissues. She gulped air and opened her eyes. Who—why wasn't she alone? She was always alone in her nightmares—but Matt was there, sitting on the edge of her bed, his arms around her. Matt.

'Oh,' she gasped. 'Oh! I've wakened you.'

He shook his head wordlessly, then dried her neck with little dabbing movements as if she was a small child. 'You had a nightmare, Leila. I heard you scream and dashed in here, thinking you were being attacked by some intruder or something. But you were fast asleep. I had to waken you, but you fought me.'

'I thought you were somebody stopping me,' she said simply.

'Stopping you? From going somewhere?'

'No. From getting help.' She looked at him properly now.

He must have switched on the lamp when he tried to wake her. His hair was tousled from sleep and his face—she looked again—his face seemed all bone and no flesh, the skin pale as parchment. 'I'm sorry, Matt, for giving you such a shock. It's usually somebody stopping me going into the sea, or me trying to pull him out and not being strong enough. I'm all right now.'

'Usually?' he asked. 'Do you mean you often have nightmares like that?'

'Not so often now. I had a lot—at first. Don't look so worried, Matt. Honestly, they're getting less frequent.'

'Have you had advice—help—about them?'

'From a doctor you mean, or a psychiatrist? No.' She shook her head. 'Nobody knows about them but you. I'm always alone, you see.'

He looked at her, a great sadness in the clear depths of his eyes. 'And they're always about Lance?'

'Yes,' she said simply.

She thought she heard him sigh and from a distance of only inches she saw the firm, beautiful mouth turn downwards and tighten. On anyone else she would have said that their lips drooped, but on Matt such a description just didn't apply.

Outside her window day was breaking to the full clamour of the dawn chorus. They must have been asleep less than an hour.

'I'm sorry you thought I was being attacked,' she said, intent on making him feel better. His bare, hairy chest was almost touching her face, while his left arm still supported her. She looked down and saw that he had come rushing to her room just as he'd slept, completely naked. Not a flicker of sexual awareness touched her, it just seemed infinitely comforting to have a man so eager to defend her that he ran into her room without a stitch of clothing.

She yawned, laid her head against his chest and said sleepily, 'Thanks, Matt.' She felt him gather her up and climb into the bed, then sit against the pillows with her on his lap. Strong arms were round her, a warm chest against her cheek, and she went to sleep cradled by a naked, black-haired man who held her as gently as a baby.

CHAPTER ELEVEN

WARM sunshine fell across her bed and from outside came the sound of a lawn-mower. Children called and somewhere a radio was playing. Leila sat up in bed and stretched. She felt marvellous.

Remembrance of the night dropped into her mind complete and entire, like the unabridged version of a film projected at high speed. She stared incredulously at her pillows as if expecting to find Matt still there, and then jumped out and snatched up her robe.

She found the door of the other bedroom open, the bed stripped and the duvet rolled back. She ran down the staircase but the sun-drenched flat was deserted. He'd gone.

She made for the kitchen. Of course he'd gone. It was after eleven and he was hardly one to sleep late when he had work to do. But she'd hoped for another talk with him, a final sorting out of their differences; she'd hoped to explain about her nightmares and to thank him for his comforting presence in the night. No more than that. Her resolve of the evening before, when she finally admitted she loved him, was as strong as ever. Another deep involvement was just not to be considered!

She put the kettle on and poured herself a glass of fruit juice, then wandered to the front window to make sure that his car *had* gone. She smiled and shook her head slowly. There weren't many women who could say they'd been to bed for the first time with the man they loved and nothing had happened, if you could call comfort and concern and caring nothing. It all seemed a bit unreal in the bright light of morning; the way he'd been there when she came out of the nightmare; the absence of any sexuality between them, and finally the way she'd gone straight to sleep in his arms, her head against his chest. Usually, after a nightmare she tossed and turned for ages, unable to throw off the horror of

134

it, but it seemed that Matt's presence had made her feel safe, secure.

She turned to go back to the kitchen and saw the note on her desk. It was written on a sheet from her small sketch-pad and was placed under a narrow glass vase holding three Josephine Bruce roses. The writing was big, straight and forceful.

Dear Leila,

I'm truly sorry to leave without talking to you again, but I've promised to be at the by-pass site by 8 a.m.

I hope you feel none the worse for your 'ghastly' time at Cowpers? Will you accept a belated apology for what I implied about Rob? I had a reason of sorts for saying it—perhaps one day soon I'll tell you what it was. See you at work, probably Tuesday, Best wishes,

                                     Matt.

Leila sat there holding the sheet of paper very carefully, as if it might disintegrate in her hands. Then she read it again. As a first letter from the man she loved it was something of a disappointment. No word of affection—just 'Best Wishes' . . . No mention of the fact that he'd been in her bed, no word about the nightmare. She remembered his face in the lamplight; grey, skull-like, shaken. Perhaps he preferred to forget it if he could. She'd probably been an unnerving sight, screaming and sobbing and wrestling with unseen dream-figures.

She folded the letter neatly and placed it in her top drawer, then went to make coffee. The situation was what she wanted, wasn't it? Back on friendly terms. No emotions, no physical desire, no rushing off and making reckless, ill-considered moves. Just mutual respect and friendship. It was a sobering thought.

Down in the garden next door she could see Dee weeding the flowerbeds. Leila watched her friend with affection, and felt a sudden need for her calm, sensible company. They had planned to have a cold lunch together in Dee's flat, as Sam was on duty, so she finished her coffee, had a shower, put on a cotton sun-dress, and then went downstairs.

Dee laid aside her trowel and brought out two canvas chairs. 'I was just trying to find a valid excuse to stop working,' she admitted. 'We can sit here in the sun for a while before lunch. How was last night? I saw that great big hunk of manhood arrive to pick you up.'

'It was a very swish do, you'd have loved it. The house is superb and the food was delicious. The grounds looked beautiful and they had a full dance band, a fire-eater, a limbo-dancer and a knife-thrower.'

'No trapeze artists?' asked Dee, laughing. 'It sounds more like a circus.'

'The entertainment *was* a bit different,' agreed Leila. 'But it was well organised and must have cost the earth. I didn't enjoy it, though. Arlene was there with Bernard, and she made it clear that she didn't want me around. Martin Deeds, the architect for the leisure centre, was there as well. I don't like him and he doesn't like me. Pete Larkin was drinking like a fish, and I had to tell him I thought the foundations of the main hall were wrong, and——'

'The foundations?' Dee pounced on that aspect at once. 'He's a civil engineer isn't he? Surely he knows what he's doing?'

Briefly, Leila told her about it. 'I'll show you the plans later, and you'll see what I mean,' she concluded.

'Tell me to get lost if you like,' said Dee, 'but, Leila, I saw him leave your place this morning. Sam and I were having breakfast.' She looked intently at her long, slender feet and moved her toes in a circular motion. 'You aren't getting any ideas there, are you? The last time we spoke of him you didn't know anything about him, not even if he was married.'

Leila was deeply touched. 'You needn't look so concerned, love. I'm not going overboard for any man ever again like I did for Lance. That was infatuation, a sort of madness really. It acted on the impulsive streak in my nature and led to—well you know what it led to.'

Dee was worried that she'd started sleeping with

Matt! Leila would have found that laughable if it hadn't been painful.

'We had to take Pete Larkin home because he'd drunk too much,' she explained. 'I drove his car back and Matt put him to bed. By the time we got here it was four o'clock. He slept in the spare bedroom and went on his way hours ago—as you saw—while I was still fast asleep.'

Relieved, Dee laughed ruefully. 'I'm sorry, but you do seem to bring out the protective instinct in me. I just don't want to see you get hurt again, that's all.'

'I know. Don't worry, it won't happen. And for your information he isn't married, but all his brothers and sisters are, and he lives in a thatched cottage outside Coventry with his mother.'

'Oh,' said Dee faintly, 'he doesn't look like a man who would live in a thatched cottage with his *mother*.'

'I know. But he does,' said Leila. With that she changed the subject. Not even to Dee could she speak of how she felt about Matt. It was something she must deal with by herself.

She was having a break on Monday morning when Pete Larkin knocked at the open door.

'Oh, good morning. Come in. I'm just having some coffee, would you like some?' She knew she was gabbling. Small wonder when she thought of their last meeting.

'Yes. Thanks.'

'Won't you sit down, Mr Larkin?'

He shook his head, but said, 'Call me Pete.'

'Oh. Right.' She smiled at him warmly, attempting to hide the fact that she felt extremely awkward. 'And you must call me Leila.'

He removed the hard hat and ran his fingers through the thick, greying hair. 'How do you like this office?' As an opener it could have been worse.

'I like it well enough. It's comfortable and convenient. But at first I was a bit embarrassed by something so luxurious. The Cowpers provided it without my knowledge, you see.'

'So Matt told me.' She thought the hard blue eyes held a more gentle expression than usual, but waited to see what came next. He finished the mug of coffee, and still standing there accepted another. 'I believe I'm indebted to you for driving my car home,' he said suddenly. 'I made a fool of myself, didn't I?'

'It could happen to anyone, Pete,' she said, studiously non-committal.

He rocked back and forth, shifting his feet uneasily. 'It was good of you. Thanks,' he managed at last.

'That's all right. The roads were quiet and I enjoyed the drive. All I did was see to the car.' She didn't want him thinking she'd helped put him to bed.

'I know. Matt told me. I managed to get hold of him on the phone late last night.'

She saw dull red colour mounting beneath the weather-beaten skin. He was starting again. 'Leila—I'm afraid I wasn't very pleasant when you told me about the footings for the main hall.'

'No. But I didn't even know if my ideas were right.'

'Oh, they were right. I've got the men altering it now. No doubt they think I'm an incompetent devil. But Matt's away for a couple of days and with any luck it'll be done before he gets back.' He swung round and stared out of the window, while Leila let relief flood through her at the outcome of her intervention. Then he said, 'I very much appreciate the fact that you told me first. Thanks.'

'Forget it. It was just luck that I happened to notice it and even more lucky that the men hadn't got any further.'

But still he wasn't finished. 'I hadn't realised I was letting my personal worries affect the job. Now I know about it I'll be on my guard. Matt has enough on his mind without another site-agent causing trouble.' She glanced at him curiously. What did he mean by that?

'One more thing then I've done.' He looked straight into her eyes. 'I know I've been as awkward as hell with you up to now, partly because I was fed up with women in general, but mainly because I didn't think you were up to the job. You've shown me that you are, and I've realised that I'm not. I apologise for any trouble and worry I've caused you.'

Leila was embarrassed. 'Thanks, Péte, but please don't say any more about it. Perhaps we can be friends now.' She held out her hand and he enclosed it with a hard beefy grip.

He smiled and nodded, then rammed the protective hat back on his head. 'I'll be off then,' he said, obviously relieved that he'd accomplished his series of apologies and thank-yous. Once again she felt that odd affinity with him. She couldn't name it but there was something there, something about him that touched a chord of sympathy and understanding in her.

The days passed; busy days. The specialist sub-contractors began dredging the lake and forming the base of the little island; another firm presented plans for the laying of the tennis courts, and Leila prepared to organise the clearing out of the overgrown elders and hawthorns around the playing fields.

It unnerved her to find how much she looked forward to Matt's return. For three days there had been no sign of him, then, as she slowed for the motorway exit one morning, she saw the helicopter on the playing fields. Her heart leapt wildly. Ridiculously, her mind began planning a dialogue with him; what he would say, how she would answer. She would be calm and friendly when they met; as different as could be from the frenzied creature he'd dealt with at daybreak in her bedroom.

As she crossed the duckboards he was leaving his caravan, his expression sombre, deep in thought. He saw her and came across. The smile flashed out and her heart jolted for the second time in minutes. 'Leila—how are you?'

'Fine thanks, Matt. And——'

'You found my note?'

'Yes. And, Matt——'

He interrupted her again. 'I can't stop, Leila. I'm sorry. I've just had an urgent phone call. I don't know when I'll be back. I may live at home for a few days within reach of the office. Pete will know where to find me.'

'Fine,' she said pleasantly. 'I'll see you some time, then.'

For an instant he looked indecisive. Only for an instant, then he strode off to the helicopter, leaving her standing there. So much for a dialogue between them! She'd been deliberately snubbed, but Matt wasn't like that. He was reasonable. He was considerate. Something was worrying him.

She stood in front of her cabin as the helicopter flew over, gaining height. It was all she could do to prevent herself waving goodbye. Spare him the fond farewells, she told herself firmly.

Later that morning Rob rang her. 'Leila? At last! I tried three times yesterday but there was no reply. Where were you?'

She was tempted to tell him that her whereabouts were none of his business, but restrained herself. 'I was out on the site, Rob. That's my job, remember?'

'Sorry. Sorry. I'm ringing to find out what you'd like to do next Saturday.'

'Next Saturday?' she repeated, puzzled.

'Your birthday. Or had you forgotten?'

'No, I hadn't, actually. I'm surprised though, that you should know when it is.'

'You put all your particulars on the entry form for the competition.'

'So I did,' she agreed resignedly.

'Well, how do you fancy a weekend in Paris? Dad says we can go over in the Lear on Saturday morning.'

'A Lear jet?'

'What else. It belongs to the Foundation, but it's kept at home so Dad can come the heavy about who uses it.'

'But—you don't pilot it, do you Rob?'

'Not yet,' he said blithely. 'Give me time—I haven't got my licence yet. Look—I've booked us a couple of rooms—a *couple*, please note—in a hotel on the Champs Elysées.'

'Have you really?' said Leila, slightly nettled. 'I thought you said just now that you were ringing to *find out* what I wanted to do?'

'Well, yes, that's right. I just booked the rooms on

the off-chance. It seemed like a good idea. Oh hell—
don't say you don't want to go.'

That was exactly what she would say if she was
honest but she couldn't be so ungracious. It was quite a
relief to be able to say, 'I'm sorry, Rob, but I've already
made arrangements to go out with somebody for the
day.'

'Oh—marvellous,' he said disgustedly. 'Parnell, I
suppose?'

'No—not Matt. It's a friend of mine and her
husband. They're taking me for a picnic near Stratford
and then to the theatre to see *Twelfth Night*.'

'A threesome?' He sounded incredulous.

'Yes. A threesome. With Dee, my best friend, and her
husband. I'm looking forward to it enormously.'

'Oh well—what about lunch one day next week? I
could pick you up at the site and take you back there.'

It was more than she could do to refuse again. 'I can
manage Thursday,' she said at last. 'I'll change here at
the office.'

'Great. I'll book a table at the Celebrity, and call for
you about twelve-thirty. And Leila—keep Sunday free,
will you?'

'I'm sorry, Rob. I'm going home for the day. I fixed
that up some time ago.'

'I should have rung before,' he said gloomily. 'Still,
see you next Thursday.'

After she'd hung up Leila perched on her work-
bench, feeling she'd had a narrow escape. A high-
powered weekend with Rob in a city packed with
tourists? No thank you.

'Pete, is everything all right with Parnell's? Matt seems
to be rushing around like a man demented.'

It was a sign of the improvement in their relationship
that she could ask such a question openly. Pete lounged
in the other armchair, drinking coffee. 'Matt doesn't tell
me everything that goes on,' he said soberly. 'My job is
to run this site in his absence, and when we talk, it's
usually about the work here; but I do know he's been
having problems with that by-pass job. The site-agent

over there has let him down badly. Not only that, there's been thieving going on—big stuff, not just petty theft.'

Leila sat opposite him. No wonder Matt hadn't time for idle conversations. She began to see more clearly his enormous responsibilities. Half-a-dozen sites around the Midlands and at each he needed a reliable man in charge. She was more glad than ever that she hadn't gone to him about the mistake in the foundations.

'Matt will cope,' went on Pete. 'He hasn't a degree or diploma to his name, but is he bright! He knows his stuff and he's as straight as they come. When I was taking my degree he was a sixteen-year-old labourer on a building site in Walsall. Think of that, then look at him now.'

Leila did think of it. She'd thought of it frequently since Matt's revelations a week ago. Everything she learned about him added to her regard. She almost wished she could hear something bad, something to despise, to dislike. Life would be a little easier if she didn't admire him as well as love him.

Pete was becoming positively talkative all at once. 'Do you know he was the only person I told when Joy left me? I couldn't bring myself to mention it to my parents or my sisters. But I told Matt. He was damn good about it.' He turned the empty coffee mug over and over in his square, capable hands, and said abruptly, 'I'm taking the kids out tomorrow.'

'Oh, I'm glad.' Leila had learned something of his problems during the last few days. He seemed to find relief in passing a remark here and there, but he did it reluctantly, as if the need to talk was in perpetual conflict with his natural reticence.

'What are you planning to do?' she asked with interest.

He managed a smile. 'Warwickshire are playing Somerset this weekend. They're both mad on cricket, so pray for sunshine. If we don't go to Edgbaston I'll probably take them to the N.E.C. to the computer exhibition. There's a special section for children.'

'Their mother doesn't—raise any objections to you

taking them out?' Leila asked gently. She hated to probe but was convinced that Pete needed to air his problems rather than brood about them.

'No, why should she?' he asked defensively. 'They're my children as well, aren't they? As a matter of fact, she's very co-operative where they're concerned, but when it comes to us—the two of us—she doesn't say much.'

'Do you?' asked Leila. 'Do you say much?'

'No,' he said abruptly, making for the door. 'What is there to say? She left me for this—this salesman. There's not much *to* say about that, is there, except when do we go for the divorce?'

He marched out. Leila sighed; he was desperately unhappy, but two ten-minute sessions a day with him were as much as she could cope with.

She picked up her notes and drawings ready to take them home. She'd planned a quiet weekend at the flat, working on sketches, listing trees and shrubs for the banks of the lake, and having a long, therapeutic session on the big water-colour of the completed site.

She was stacking her stuff in the XJS when the Range Rover drew up at the main gate. She stood by the car, ready for a casual word in passing, but at the sight of his face she almost ran towards him. 'Matt—you look awful! Aren't you well? Can I help?'

He looked exhausted. His face was grey with fatigue and the eyes, usually so clear and alert, were deep-sunk in their sockets. Blue-black stubble shadowed his jaw and his lips were set tightly. 'Leila,' he said gently. 'I'm all right, don't fuss.' Even the voice was altered. It was flat, weary, dog-tired.

'I—thought something had happened,' she said hesitantly.

'Something *has* happened,' he agreed. 'I've given three of my top men the sack, that's what's happened. That, and a lot of other things, all equally unpleasant.'

'Oh, how awful. Can I help?' she asked again.

'I don't think so. I've got somebody coming in a minute who'll be able to help me quite a bit, though.'

It was a dismissal, gentle but unmistakable.

'Well, I'll be off then.' She managed a smile and resisted the urge to touch his hand. She left him heading for the caravan and saw Jacob hurry out with a covered plate. Once more she saw a distinct similarity between the attitude of the crop-haired ex-navvy and that of Agnes.

At the top of the road she passed a silver Porsche, slowing for the turning to the site. From the driving seat Iris Hamilton waved, her black hair coiled behind her ears, gigantic gold-framed sunglasses covering her lovely eyes.

Leila waved back and went on her way. She knew now who the 'somebody who'll be able to help' was. The ache beneath her ribs increased. He sent her off home while he waited for Iris to arrive and help him. Well, that was clear enough. She'd got the message.

CHAPTER TWELVE

LEILA changed out of the ivory silk dress she'd worn for her lunch with Rob, and back into her working clothes. It had been a superb meal, and Rob had been excellent company, but as always, somewhat wearing.

Her mind went back over his non-stop talking and selected remarks that had perhaps been intended to remain with her. 'Yes, Iris is working closely with Parnell at the moment . . . She's a wizard with finances, you know—plays the markets like other people play the banjo . . . If his firm's in trouble she's the one to sort him out . . .' And most puzzling of all, 'You're paid by us, anyway, not Parnells.'

She'd stayed non-committal, refusing to be drawn, but the outwardly casual comments had been both worrying and reassuring. If Matt was indeed seeing Iris purely in her professional capacity then that was reassuring, but she felt sick with worry that his firm might be in deep trouble.

She buttoned her pink shirt and then on impulse went to the phone. Dobbs could find out for her if it was true. But—no—no—she could hardly ring from the Parnell site to ask for confidential information about Parnell affairs. She'd go home early and call at his office.

Later, she set off for the playing fields, ready to mark those trees and shrubs which were too far gone to be retained, and as she went reflected that it hadn't even occurred to her to ask Matt himself about it. If he'd wanted her to know, he'd have told her. But he hadn't said a word. He'd just gone into a huddle with Iris, the financial wizard.

Dragging her mind back to the job, she looked down and felt a spurt of pleasure at the sight of the grass beneath her feet. The football pitches wouldn't have to be re-laid from scratch. With intensive care the turf could be up-graded and made fit for use by the time the leisure-centre opened. With strips of red hessian she went along the hedging and marked those shrubs which were to be removed.

The noise of the helicopter sliced through the comparative quiet of the playing fields. It landed so near that the wind from the blades caught at her shirt and whipped her hair from its loose top-knot. When the engine was switched off the everyday sounds could be heard again. The constant hum of traffic from the motorway, the two-tone note of a diesel far away along the railway line, the chugging of cement mixers.

She hadn't seen Matt to speak to since that brief exchange a week ago, and she was so glad to see him that she almost ran towards him. 'Hello, Matt,' she beamed. 'How are you?'

He looked down at her. The thick honey-gold hair swirled around in wild disarray, her smooth golden cheeks were tinged with colour, her eyes bright with the excitement of seeing him unexpectedly.

'I'm a bit happier than the last time we met,' he said, laughing. 'But then I didn't know I'd get such a welcome!'

'I just happened to be out here marking the hedging ready for clearing. Pete says he'll put some men on it on Monday.'

'Oh—it's "Pete" now? That sounds as if the two of you are on better terms.'

'Yes. We're friends now,' she said simply.

'I'm glad.' His mouth curved upwards and she found herself anticipating the smile, but she was disappointed. 'Leila,' he said seriously. 'I'm sorry it's been so long since I saw you to speak to, but things have been pretty hectic.' He looked at his watch, glanced keenly towards the bulldozers on the skyline and then asked, 'Have you an hour to spare?'

'Yes,' she said promptly.

'I wondered if you'd like to have a look at some of the sites from the helicopter? For ages I've been thinking it might interest you. What do you say? We won't land, just hover for a minute or two then on to the next one.'

'I'd love it,' she said at once.

In moments they were airborne, heading east. Neither of them spoke for long moments. Matt seemed occupied with his own thoughts, and Leila was busy comparing this trip with the previous one when he took her to the coral island.

As always, she was thrilled by the superb views from on high. It was fascinating to see the aerial aspect of roads that were familiar to her only at ground level. Before long, he banked and turned, then kept the machine hovering above a small estate of forty private houses. 'Oh, that's a good lay-out,' she breathed. 'They look expensive, Matt, are they all sold?'

'No, not yet,' he said regretfully. 'They're going at £85,000 plus. Several months ago we had a provisional waiting list, but people have backed out recently. The first two are finished and the tenants are moving in next week.'

'You've been able to keep all the mature trees?' Leila noted with intense interest several fine specimens among the houses.

'Only half-a-dozen had to be lost on the entire site,' he admitted, with that sideways lift of the mouth. 'The land was divided according to the trees, not the houses. It's meant that the size of the gardens varies an awful lot, but that seems to suit most people.'

The next site was within three miles. A local authority development of bungalows and maisonettes for the elderly. Leila peered down intently and saw some of the workers look up and wave. 'Boss-man is watching!' she teased.

'Yes. They'll wonder why Boss-man isn't landing,' he laughed. 'Things are going well there. One of my best gangs of brickies are working like mad. We'll have the roofs on the bungalows in less than a week.'

They whirled away then to one of the series of small boroughs which run into each other on the outer edges of the Birmingham area. 'That's the by-pass,' he said, seriously now.

'It's huge!' Leila was astounded. 'I didn't imagine anything of that size.'

'Yes. It's big,' he agreed, staring down at the long scar of the new road across the smooth green skin of the fields.

Leila thought that the amount of heavy machinery in use was prodigious. 'Is everything under control again down there?' she asked, fixing her gaze, for some reason, on Matt's brawny forearms.

As she'd somehow expected, he was evasive. 'Things are gradually settling down again. Don't worry your head about it, Leila.'

'Don't worry your head, little woman,' she thought bitterly. 'Don't think of anything that might tax that little bird-brain.' The remark, and the implication behind it, came oddly from the tolerant and liberal-minded man at her side. Did he really think her mental equipment so lightweight that she couldn't take in details of his troubles with the by-pass? She bit her lip and kept silent, reluctant to disturb the rapport between them.

He headed north-west next, handling the controls with evident pleasure, and she realised then that the powerful little machine meant a great deal to him. 'The next one is the last in this area,' he said. 'There are three more—two in the Nottingham district and one near Leicester, but we'll have to look at those some other time.'

They hovered above a single-storey building set in immaculate playgrounds and playing fields. Even from above she could see the distinctive grace of the buildings, the unusual layout. Matt couldn't quite conceal his pride when he said, 'A new junior school for three hundred pupils finished about six weeks ago.'

'It's lovely, Matt,' she said, squirming round in her seat to get a better view. 'Who was the architect?'

'Martin Deeds,' he said. 'Do you still say it's lovely?'

'Oh yes. He's a good architect. I admit it. I don't have to like him as well, do I?'

Matt smiled. 'No. He's an oddity, is Martin. But it might interest you to know that the last time I was talking to him he came very close to admitting that you knew your job.'

'Did he indeed? He showed no signs of it at the Cowper barbecue,' she said wryly. 'He was a perfect horror when I was dealing with those two men from the Bequest Committee.'

'Martin is a law unto himself. Don't let him get you down.' He swung the machine round to start the return journey.

'All your projects are superb, Matt,' she said sincerely. 'I've really loved seeing them from up here.'

He shot her a glance, the grey eyes almost transparently clear. 'Good. I thought you might.'

Mention of the barbecue had inevitably brought to Leila's mind the events which had followed it. 'Matt,' she said slowly, 'this is the first chance I've had to say anything, but I'd like to thank you for putting up with me when I had that nightmare, and for being such— such a comfort.'

He stretched out a big hand and covered hers warmly for an instant. 'Forget it,' he said. 'Have you had one since then?'

'No,' she said with some relief. 'It's the longest spell without one that I've had so far. Perhaps you've banished them for good!'

'Let's hope so,' he said gently, and then, with a slight hardening of the deep voice, he said, 'I gather Rob Cowper is still not taking "No" for an answer?'

'What? Oh—well, I've been out to lunch with him today, if that's what you mean.'

'No,' he said drily. 'I was thinking of your weekend trip to Paris. My helicopter is pretty small beer compared to a private jet, I imagine.'

She stared at him. 'Rob told you we were going to Paris?'

'No. As a matter of fact it was Iris who mentioned it.'

She eyed his dark profile. Seen against the pale sky it had a disdainful look against it that she didn't care for. 'I see,' she said edgily. 'And you think your helicopter doesn't compare very favourably with the Lear?'

'The idea did occur to me,' he said evenly.

For a moment Leila was silent. 'When you report back to your lady friend perhaps you'd give her the facts,' she said grimly, 'not that I think my activities are any of her business. A week ago Rob asked me to fly with him to Paris on Saturday. I refused at once as I had a previous engagement with my best friend and her husband. I would still have refused if I hadn't had a previous engagement. Rob doesn't like to take "No" for an answer, but sometimes he has to.'

'Oh,' said Matt. It was the first time she'd seen him at a loss. 'Leila—what can I say? I had no reason to doubt what Iris told me.'

She heard her voice put into words what was only a half-formed impression in her mind. 'I think Iris likes to work things her way—to get what she wants. She and Rob are very alike in that, I imagine.'

Matt nodded thoughtfully. 'What Iris wants, she usually gets. But in this case she was merely mistaken. I do apologise, Leila. It seems as if something about Rob Cowper leads me to make rash judgments.'

They were silent while the helicopter racketed across the sky towards the still unseen motorway and the site. Leila sat there, shaken. The exchange of the last few minutes had shown her one thing, and that with absolute clarity. The fragile little barriers she'd been at pains to erect against her feelings for Matt were quite useless. It was futile to say she mustn't get involved. She *was* involved, and she wanted to get even *more* involved. She loved him.

With a supreme effort she threw off her resentment, and began to tell him about Dee and Sam. About the day she moved into the flat and found them living next door; and about Dee being a fellow student in landscape design. 'She'd like to come and see over the site sometime, Matt. Would that be all right?'

She could tell by the way he looked at her that he knew she'd made an effort to get back on good terms. 'Of course it would,' he said. 'Any time. I'd like to meet her.'

Leila touched the instrument panel with the tips of her fingers. 'Actually, I prefer this to an executive jet.'

He handled the controls lightly, an odd expression on his face. 'Look your last on it then, and say a fond farewell. I'm selling it.'

'Matt! You use it such a lot. How can you bear to part with it?'

'It wasn't new when I bought it, but there's plenty of life in the blades, and I've been offered forty thousand for it. That's how I can bear to part with it.' Once again the message was there, pleasant but unmistakable: 'Don't pry. The company is my affair.'

The motorway was almost below them, the traffic nose to tail in the evening build-up. He landed on the playing fields, and when he switched off the engine the site was silent, the men gone home.

He came round to lift her down, the high bank of overgrown shrubs behind him. The sound of the traffic was muted now, and that one green corner of the site held an illusion of solitude.

He reached up for her, his hands on either side of her waist, but he didn't set her down. Instead he pulled her to his chest, while her toes swung six inches from the grass. Then he bent his dark hard and kissed her.

It was so quick, so unexpected, that her breath was expelled through her parted lips and sighed into his mouth. That beautiful mouth ... It was warm and sweet and demanding on hers. Her mind reeled in amazement even as her senses wakened to the excitement of being in his arms. Without taking his mouth from hers he allowed her feet to touch the ground, and she felt his hands, big and hard, flat on her back below her shoulder blades.

Her arms went up round his neck, and her fingers into his hair. Why had she ever imagined she knew what kissing was like when she'd never been kissed by Matt? Lips parted, her heart full of love, she kissed him back, stretching up on tip-toe as she felt his thighs against her hips, the hardness of him searching for refuge.

In the close-folded circle of his arms she was pliant, weak with desire. She forgot that he'd shown no previous sign of loving her, wanting her, and when he lifted his lips from hers she sighed, suddenly bereft that his mouth was gone. But he was kissing her throat, the little satin-skinned hollow where her gold chain lay warm against the damp skin.

His fingers moved to the buttons of her shirt, and wordlessly she thrust forward her breasts, aching for him to touch them. It no longer registered that only the helicopter lay between them and the homegoing crowds on the motorway. Her senses ruled that they were alone, up among the silvering clouds.

She felt the fabric of her shirt ease as he undid the buttons. 'Leila,' he said softly, 'I can't resist you, although I know I should . . .' She felt his breath waft against her hair as the third button was undone.

'Matt! I say, Matt? Are you there?' It was Larkin's voice, loud and impatient. Matt released her, and she saw on his face both anger and surprise. Later she was to ponder exactly who or what had caused each emotion. Now, he moved in front of her, while she fastened her shirt. A moment later Pete Larkin appeared round the high hedge. 'Oh, Matt. Miss Hamilton's on the phone for you. She's rung twice already, and been on to the other sites as well. She says it's urgent.'

Matt turned to Leila. 'I'm sorry,' he said quietly. The three of them walked back to the huts together, Matt and Pete discussing details of the buildings, while Leila tried to bring order to the chaos of her thoughts. For a few heart-shaking moments, she'd thought that Matt felt deeply about her, that he wanted her beyond the physical urge which had rocked them both a moment ago. Now, he was apologising for it having happened. What was she to make of that?

They reached the caravan. Again she glimpsed some conflict of emotions on his face, then he turned, and without another word went to speak to Iris on the phone.

Back in her cabin, Leila gathered up her things and then went home. It was still early, but she didn't want to see Matt again until she'd decided for herself just what had been behind that interlude out on the fields. With a strained smile and a wave to Pete, she made for the car.

The raspberries hung jewel-like from the canes. Leila

moved along the orderly rows, opposite Agnes, filling
the basket and popping one into her mouth now and
again. It was hot and tranquil in the big, netted fruit-
cage at Ardenfields, and Leila submitted with good
grace to the housekeeper's interrogation, knowing that
in her own way, Agnes cared more for her than for
anyone else on earth.

'Matt? Oh yes, he's all right, Agnes. By the way, he
didn't come to view the house as a prospective home for
him and Iris Hamilton, it's her parents who are house-
hunting.

'Oh aye? She looked to me as if she was the one ready
for a place of her own,' said Agnes shrewdly, 'and I'd
not have any trouble guessing who she'd like to share it
with, either.' She topped up the basket neatly. 'I expect
your friends next door would like some? And Maisie is
freezing plenty so that you can take a pack home
whenever you call. She's jamming tonight, so there'll be
a few pots of that in the larder for you as well.'

'Making jam on a Sunday evening?' asked Leila.
'Isn't that pushing it a bit? Why can't she relax after
tea?'

'She can if she wants to,' declared Agnes. 'But we
didn't pick any yesterday, knowing that it's something
you like doing.'

Leila leaned across the serrated leaves and planted a
kiss on Agnes's cheek. There were times when she was
moved almost to tears by their thoughtfulness. 'If you
want to sunbathe I've got one of those bikinis you left
behind——' Agnes sniffed, not very delicately '—and
your special place is all ready in the rose garden. We
thought you might like to have tea outside, so shall we
put the sun umbrella out on the big lawn?'

She waddled away carrying the basket of raspberries
like a trophy, while Leila went to change. It still felt
strange to come to the house as a visitor, and she
dreaded it being handed over to new owners.

Later, she lay on the lounger, letting the warm
English sun soak into skin that had known far hotter
days under the brazen skies of Australia, and in the
steaming heat of Thailand. Arlene was in London with

Bernard, viewing apartments in Belgravia. Leila wondered what her stepmother thought of the London property market. Was she staggered by the prices or did she accept them and juggle her finances accordingly?

She hadn't expected Arlene to remember her birthday, but she had still felt that foolish twinge of regret when she didn't get so much as a card. As it turned out, though, she'd had a lovely day. Leila lay among the roses and looked back on it with pleasure. There weren't many cards; she had no family and the friends who at one time would have remembered, were out of touch after her long spell abroad with Lance, but there had been cards and presents from Agnes and Maisie and Jack, a funny card from Dee and Sam showing a harrassed woman trying to plant a tree; even a small unobtrusive one from Pete Larking bearing the message, 'Regards and thanks—Pete'. Unsure what the thanks were for she'd decided they could only be for providing a listening ear.

It had been no surprise to receive a huge boxed card from Rob, but at least it had been a lighthearted one, with no protestations of affection other than the line of crosses above the large scrawled signature. His box of red roses had arrived before nine o'clock—twenty-six of them, evidence that he'd checked the year of her birth as well as the date.

Foolish to have imagined that Matt might have sent her a card. There was no way he could have known it was her birthday unless Rob or even Iris had told him. She had swallowed her disappointment and arranged the lovely roses.

The outing with Dee and Sam was their present to her and they had done things in style. A delicious picnic lunch, eaten on a grassy bank overlooking the Avon; cold chicken and salad, white wine and a spectacular orange gateau made by Dee. It had been a wonderful birthday meal, with Sam teasing them both, his bald head shining and his vivid blue eyes constantly turned on his wife.

Then they had visited Dee's home. A houseful of brothers and sisters, nieces and nephews, all coming

and going throughout the afternoon; Dee's mother in
the kitchen making innumerable pots of tea, and her
father pottering in the garden with one ear cocked for
the cricket commentary. It was a novel experience for
Leila to be with a large family group, and once or twice
she had to pull herself up sharply before she fell into
undisguised envy of her friend.

The performance of *Twelfth Night* was scintillating.
Within minutes, though, Leila found that her attention
was not wholly taken up by the play. Her mind kept
wandering obstinately along paths which led only to
Matt, then back again to the stage on hearing some
familiar line. When Viola, on stage, pleaded her
master's suit to Olivia, saying, 'Make me a willow cabin
at your gate, and call upon my soul within the house,'
Leila thought instantly of her own cabin at the gate of
the site, and looked at Dee with a rueful smile. But the
allusion was lost on her; she was holding hands with
Sam and all their attention was focused on the stage. It
was a strange sensation to be watching one of her
favourite plays, yet to have her mind leaping about
elsewhere, out of her control ... Still, it had been a
lovely birthday.

It was hot for an English July. Leila listened to the
bees in the low lavender hedge, and pondered on the
letter she'd received from Mr Dobbs. He had moved
fast. Delivered by hand, the letter had been waiting for
her when she got home from work on Friday evening.

Dear Miss Garland,
In answer to your enquiry I have obtained the
following information from reliable sources. Parnell
Enterprises is not in immediate danger of bankruptcy,
but is suffering a cash-flow problem. The business
has always been sound, but severe strain was felt at
the time of the Garland takeover, when Mr Bernard
Grover, for Garlands, drove a hard bargain.

In recent weeks a loss has been sustained on the
roadworks site, where incompetent supervision has
delayed completion, thus risking breach of contract
proceedings. Not only that, theft has occurred on a

large scale, both of equipment and raw materials. Mr Parnell has declined to prosecute the men responsible, giving as his reason the fact that he used to 'work on the same gang'.

Add to this the state of the building trade, the late payments from his customers, and the fact that the banks are reluctant to grant him more credit. Shares in the firm have been sold up to the limit beyond which Mr Parnell would lose control of the company.

The amount needed, in cash terms, is relatively small. A million would do it, maybe less, say £850,000. If this amount cannot be raised fairly soon some sites may have to be closed down and the men laid off. I may add that Miss Iris Hamilton, freelance broker, seems to be deeply involved with Mr Parnell's finances. Professionally, the lady is highly regarded.

Hoping the above may be of some use to you,

I remain, yours faithfully,

Herbert G. Dobbs.

Leila had read the letter so often she knew it by heart, but she had decided what to do about it within ten minutes of first reading it.

CHAPTER THIRTEEN

LEILA was late in arriving at the site on Monday morning. She'd planned to spend five minutes with Mr Dobbs, but it had taken much longer than that to overcome his mulish resistance to her instructions.

She'd won in the end, of course, because the money was hers, unconditionally. She wanted her stocks, securities and bonds to be cashed, and the resulting capital offered to Matt Parnell as an interest-free loan for an indefinite period; and the amount made up from her other accounts, to a straight half-million.

The lawyer thought she was mad, or at the very least reckless and impulsive. He'd put every obstacle he could think of in her path, and at last, eyes glacial, she'd told him that if he didn't want to do as she asked, she'd hire somebody who did. Because it would take several days to arrange, Parnells were to be told at once that the loan would shortly be available, and the name of Leila Garland was to be kept out of the negotiations.

Now, waiting for the British Rail surveyor to come and discuss her proposals for altering the railway embankment, Leila felt pleased and relieved that the loan had been set in motion. Matt needed more than she could offer, but surely her half million would help? He needed it. He could have it. She loved him.

An hour later she stood by the gate, seeing the man from the railways off the site. He'd left her with plenty to think about. She tucked the plastic-covered plan under her arm and pushed her notebook in the pocket of her donkey jacket. A thin, chilly rain was falling from a leaden sky, and she burrowed deep inside her jacket and walked back to the cabin.

'Oh—hello Pete.' She hid the fact that she didn't want to talk to him just then, and what was more, was finding it a strain to act as a one-woman marriage counsellor, and an unqualified one at that.

He hung up her wet jacket and presented her with a mug of coffee. 'Thanks. That's lovely. I've got some more of that birthday cake somewhere. Do you want a piece?'

They sat in the armchairs drinking coffee and eating cake. She could tell by his face that the meeting with his wife the previous evening hadn't gone well.

'How was Joy?'

Pete looked into his coffee mug and said abruptly, 'She's packed him in.'

'The salesman? She's left him?'

'Yes. She's living at her mother's.'

'Pete—that's marvellous news. Is she coming back to you?'

'No. Oh no. She isn't sure if she wants to. She doesn't think it will work. She doesn't know if she loves me. My God, I could have been sick listening to the drivel she talked. Leila—she—she says that I never show her I love her.'

Now they were getting down to it. Leila had often wondered how demonstrative he was—after all he was a taciturn man, not given to easy speech.

'Well—do you? Show her, I mean.'

'Of course I do,' he said, resentment tightening his jaw. 'My God, I've worked like a dog for her for years. She has the best I can afford, her own car. The kids have riding lessons, judo lessons. I help her mother pay her rates. What more can I do?'

'But, Pete—do you *tell* her you love her?'

'Oh—you're on that tack again, are you? I've told her. Yes—I've told her. In words of one syllable.'

'How often?'

'What? Oh—a few times. Several times. How often do I have to repeat it?'

'For some women, once is enough. For others, several times a day, I think.'

He was silent. 'Pete, I really do feel that if you could both arrange to go to a marriage guidance centre—I'm sure they would help you.'

He wasn't listening. 'I'm fifteen years older than Joy. Did I tell you that?'

'Yes, you did,' said Leila gently. What was coming now?

'Well, would you believe that I only ever slept with one other woman before we were married?'

'Yes,' she said carefully, 'I could believe that.' And she could. Few people would take him for a promiscuous type. As to whether he was sexy, that wasn't always so obvious.

'It was when I was a kid of twenty,' he went on. 'I sort of—sort of set women on a pedestal, you know. After that one time—and it was a disaster, I can tell you—I just waited until the right woman came along. I never wanted any woman except Joy—never. But now I can't get the idea out of my head that she's always found me a disappointment.' He swallowed painfully, 'In bed, I mean.'

'Look, Pete. We can't talk here—not properly. Why don't you come round to the flat tonight for a drink? I can't give you my full attention now. I've got to make notes on what that railway chap said, go and see Ben Ford about his schedules for next week, and lots of other things. Then I'm out 'till about eight-thirty tonight. Would you like to come round for an hour around nine? I'll find out about marriage guidance in Solihull as well. Perhaps you'll be able to persuade Joy to go with you. What do you say?'

He stood up and rammed the hat back on his head. 'All right,' he said, and managed a faint smile. 'Thanks, Leila. See you tonight then.'

She watched his broad muscular figure head for the deep trench behind the foundations of the swimming baths. She thought he was suffering from an undermining of confidence in himself as a man; his belief in his own manhood, his own virility, was badly shaken. 'Amateur psychologist,' she told herself scornfully.

Wearily she took out her notebook and started to write out in sequence the points raised by the man from British Rail. Outside the cabin the rain poured down. It ran from the edge of the verandah, it dripped from her hanging baskets, it streamed from the jib of the giant crane opposite her window.

She felt exhausted. The session with Dobbs must have taken more out of her than she'd realised. His remarks about Matt and Iris had shaken her, as well. He'd seemed convinced that there was more between them than a professional relationship. And long ago she'd judged them to be lovers, hadn't she? If that was the case, though, why hadn't Iris leapt forward with a loan? Iris, who 'played the markets like other people played the banjo'.

Now there was Pete to think about. His misery caught at her heart. She stared out of the window. The plants dripped and the rain drummed on the roof; it ran along the duckboards and filled the deep grooves left by the earth-movers. It seemed to her that the whole world was weeping.

Leila sat by the window and watched the stars fade. The man on the bed slept heavily on his back, legs slightly apart, arms by his sides, palms upwards, like a patient under a deep anaesthetic.

Wearily she turned and looked at him. The grey-streaked hair was tousled, the weather-beaten skin dark against her pale green pillows. She could see his mouth, the lips soft in sleep, unlike the hard straight line of his waking hours. She thought of another mouth, a beautiful mouth, set in a tough, battered face; a mouth which had kissed her with heart-shaking passion, and she closed her eyes at the irony of seeing the wrong man in her bed.

As they'd arranged, Pete had come to see her, wrapped in his troubles. Aided by a whisky, and then another one, he at last voiced his fears. That he would never get Joy back, that he was no good as a lover, that in fact he was somehow less than a man. She had tried to reassure him, had given him another drink and realised too late that he must have had several before he arrived. At last he agreed to ask Joy if she would go with him to see the marriage guidance people.

It was only ten-thirty when he got up to go. She saw that he swayed as he made for the door, and decided she'd have to drive him home. Then he touched her hand. She knew at once what he wanted, and cursed herself bitterly for her blindness. But how, she thought, were you supposed to know that a man wanted to take you to bed when he never stopped talking about his wife?

As they stood by the open door he lurched towards her and grabbed her by the shoulders, his lips clumsily seeking hers. Sudden fear and revulsion overcame her compassion. He was drunk, he was immensely strong, and if what he'd been saying was anything to go by he needed to prove his virility. She looked down the stairs. She couldn't possibly bundle him outside and into a car as Matt had done at the Cowpers.

Fear cleared her mind and she thought at lightning speed. Sober, Pete wouldn't do this in a thousand years. Half-drunk, he was capable of anything, of using her as a substitute for Joy, venting his hurt and humiliation on her. But *fully* drunk, he would be safe. She remembered the limp, senseless form that Matt had slung over his shoulder that night.

She shut the door. 'Let's have one more drink,' she said calmly. She poured him another whisky and added vodka instead of soda. He tossed it down, and put an arm round her waist and made for the staircase. His legs refused the winding spiral, so he pulled himself upwards solely by his arms. Humiliated, repelled, and yet desperately sorry for the man, Leila followed him with a bottle of vodka and a glass.

Already she could see his eyes glazing, but he managed one more drink, then lay back against her pillows and immediately passed out.

Relief flooded through her. What would be his reactions in the morning, she wondered. She took off his trousers and shoes, flung a sheet over him, and went off to the spare bed. But not to sleep. Hours later she made coffee, and hearing him mumbling, went in to see that he was still safely flat out. She spent the rest of the night in the chair, watching in case he suddenly made a lightning recovery.

*   *   *

Leila put only toast and grapefruit on the table, sure that Pete wouldn't want much to eat. She was dressed ready for work in clean jeans and a T-shirt; it had been more than she could face to sit opposite him in a nightie and dressing gown.

He came in, heavy-eyed and unshaven. She saw at once that he avoided her eyes as he drank black coffee. Then he pushed his plate aside, put his chin on his hands, and looked into her eyes. She recalled that once before he'd said to her what he had to say and hadn't stopped until he'd got through the lot. She poured them both another coffee then sat back and waited, wary of what was coming. He wasn't going to find this easy.

'That's the first time I've slept with anybody else since I married Joy,' he said heavily.

Leila stared at him, dumbfounded.

'I made use of you,' he stated.

He thought they'd made love! But didn't he *know*? Her mind whirled with questions, then instinct took over. 'Oh, I wouldn't put it quite like that,' she said.

'You wouldn't? Oh.' He thought for a moment, then said slowly, 'Leila, did you do it because you felt sorry for me?'

The vital question. She reminded herself urgently that it was an intelligent man who'd asked it. She dredged up every ounce of conviction she could muster. 'Sorry for you? Pete—I've often felt sorry for you since you told me about your marriage—but feeling sorry for a man doesn't make me want to go to bed with him.'

'It doesn't?' Thank goodness, there was relief there.

'No chance.' She smiled brightly. 'But it was a one-night stand, you know. I don't make a habit of sleeping with married men, however good they are.'

'Good?' He latched on to the word, and she lowered her eyes hastily. He needed as much reassurance as a teenager.

'Pete—I don't reckon to sleep around, but I'm twenty-six and I know a bit about men. You've got nothing to worry about.'

He let out his breath slowly and drank deeply of his

coffee. 'I don't remember much about it, Leila. I'd drunk quite a bit, you know.'

She felt a surge of deep resentment. He'd come to her flat, talked her to death about his marital problems, got aggressively drunk, tried to sleep with her, and now, convinced he'd managed it and that she'd been willing, he was almost disclaiming responsibility. One day, if he ever got back with Joy, she would tell him exactly what had happened . . .

He jumped up. She would have had to be blind not to see he was anxious to leave. 'I'm going now.' He touched her hand across the table. 'Thanks, Leila.'

That was it. 'Thanks, Leila' and his debt, as he saw it, was paid.

She smiled again, thinking that if she'd done nothing else she'd shifted that defeated look from behind his eyes. 'See you at the site,' she said lightly.

He went down the stairs and out to the Vauxhall, leaving her close to tears. Slowly she climbed the stairs and went into the bedroom. It smelled of sweat and stale whisky. Her stomach heaved. She opened the window wider and stripped the bed completely, her movements stiff and mechanical, like those of a robot; then took the bedding downstairs for the washing machine.

The doorbell rang as she reached the bottom of the spiral. The sound of it jerked her back to her normal speed. She hadn't got rid of him yet! What had he forgotten? Her mind skidded rapidly over what they'd said to each other. Was he going to ask her something she couldn't answer?

She opened the door, taut with tension. Matt stood there.

'Oh! It's you! What a surprise,' she said weakly. Hastily she dumped the bundle of bedding on the floor at her side.

He stared down at it and then back at her. His eyes had the dull, opaque appearance that she'd seen once or twice before. 'I—I was just getting ready to set off for work, Matt,' she gabbled. Her cheeks felt cold as death and she knew she'd lost colour.

'Did you think he'd left something behind?' he asked smoothly.

'Left——? Oh. You saw Pete?'

'Yes. I called to see you last night at about nine-thirty but I saw his Vauxhall on the drive and realised you had a visitor. So I went home and tried again this morning.'

'Oh? Well, what can I do for you? Come in and sit down.'

'No thanks,' he said shortly. 'It was nothing vital, anyway.'

'You came from Coventry—twice—for nothing vital?'

'That's right,' he said. He was looking down at the pile of bedding. 'From the expression on your face when you opened the door I gather that Pete wasn't given the spare bed?'

'No,' she said quietly. 'He wasn't, but——'

She saw his face go grey. 'What are you trying to do, woman, give his marriage the death-blow?'

'No. It's not what——'

'You're a fool!' he said savagely. 'Pete isn't the type to mess about with other women. Couldn't you see that?'

She stared at him. Dear heaven, he was angry on behalf of Pete! For a moment she'd thought—fool— idiot—*imbecile*—she'd thought he was jealous.

'Yes, I could see it,' she said, ready to explain everything. 'Over the last few weeks I've seen a lot of things. I've seen his self-confidence shattered by his wife leaving him. I've seen the worry of it affect his work. I've seen him desperate to be with his boys. I've seen him longing to see Joy, but when he did he was too inarticulate and too resentful to communicate with her.' She took a breath. 'And I've seen him believing that he's a failure in bed.'

Matt glared at her savagely. He actually bared his teeth, and she took a step backwards. 'You've evidently seen a great deal,' he said tightly. 'And you decided he needed a bit of sex-therapy. A touch of the Masters and Johnson.'

'No,' she said white-faced. 'I didn't decide any such thing. If you'll just listen for a minute——'

'No I won't,' he said flatly. 'I won't listen. I can see I was naive to imagine there was only Cowper in the running. I little knew what you meant that afternoon when you said that you and Pete were "friends".' He breathed noisily as if he'd been running and he held his hands at waist-level. They looked big and brown and dangerous, clenching and unclenching like the hands of a madman. She took another step backwards and felt her distress vanish beneath a hot surge of anger.

'Look, Matt! I don't question you as to why you sleep with Iris. It's your affair. You're a grown man, just as I'm a grown woman.'

'Iris? Oh yes. I've slept with Iris. We both enjoyed it while it lasted.' He spoke the words oddly, as if referring to a side-issue.

But Leila wasn't having any more. 'You'd better go, Matt. I always thought you a reasonable man, but you're behaving like a maniac.' She marched to the door, then the urge to explain, to justify herself, overcame her anger. 'Matt,' she began, 'I was sorry for Pete, but——'

'Sorry for him! I imagine you'd be sorry for a meths drinker in his doss-house, or a prisoner coming out of Winson Green. Are you saying you'd sleep with them as well?'

She leaned against the wall with her eyes closed. She could hardly bear to see the expression in his eyes. 'If you'll shut up for a moment and let me tell you what happened,' she said.

'There's only one thing I'd like you to tell me, and then I'm going. Has Pete laid the ghost as well as laying you?'

The crudity of it bit at her. But what did he mean? 'The ghost?' she repeated.

'The ghost of Pearson. The boyfriend. Lance. L-A-N-C-E.'

She stared at him. 'How do you mean?'

'You're supposed to be in love with him, or at least in love with his memory. Or have you forgotten?'

She rubbed her jaws with the palm of her hand. Her face felt as if it was encased in marble. 'I haven't forgotten anything about Lance. I only wish I could. But let's get one thing clear. I wasn't in love with Lance, or with his memory.'

He was quite still. 'What?'

'It's almost a year since I loved Lance and even then it wasn't real love. It was infatuation. I soon found that out.' Why was he staring at her like that? 'I never told you I loved him.'

'No,' he said carefully. 'No, you never did.' His voice was expressionless, devoid of meaning.

She opened the door. She could stand no more. 'Don't come here again,' she said wearily.

He looked at her for the space of several seconds. Then without another word he went out and down the stairs. She heard the Range Rover start up, but that was all, because she ran to the bathroom and vomited up her breakfast.

It was still and very warm in the garden. Leila sat in a canvas chair and stared emptily ahead. After Matt had gone she'd prowled the flat, unable to either sit or stand still until the washing machine finished its cycle, because she was obsessed with the need to free the sheets and pillowcases of her bed from what she now saw as the contamination of Pete's drunken presence. Snatching up the damp washing, she rushed down to hang it out to dry in the garden, then hovered restlessly until it was dry.

All at once she snatched it from the line and bundled it into one of the dustbins. Then she felt better. She fell to weeding the flowerbeds, her mind dwelling on each word of the bitter exchange with Matt. She had no way of knowing whether she'd been right or wrong in letting Pete think he'd slept with her. Perhaps she'd been an idiot to follow the instinct that had urged her to try and restore his confidence? Time would tell.

It was Matt who concerned her now. He'd been furious . . . livid . . . almost beside himself. He'd known Pete for years and was doubtless as concerned about his marriage as she was. She reminded herself that she didn't hold a monopoly on worrying about it.

But—what had brought him to her flat twice in ten hours? The idea that it had been something to do with his money troubles lodged firmly at the front of her mind and refused to be moved. She might never find out now. She'd shown him the door and said 'Don't come here again.' He would hardly take that as an invitation to come and tell her his troubles.

As for the proposed loan of the half million, she saw no reason to change her plans about that. Mr Dobbs must go ahead and do as she'd demanded. Matt wouldn't know who had offered it, and it might help him through a very sticky patch.

She faced the fact that the friendship between them was over. That magical, other-worldly interlude after the helicopter trip might never have happened. He'd obviously acted on impulse, and she hoped he would think the same about her response. She still had her work to think of; the job for Cowpers must be done to the best of her ability. At peace with herself at last, Leila fell fast asleep in the secluded garden.

'Are you all right, Leila? You seem a bit subdued.' Dee was looking at her closely, and Leila wondered how much she saw, how much she guessed.

'I've had a day off work, and spent it in the garden. I felt I needed a break, that's all.'

Dee seemed unconvinced. 'I don't want to pry—but you seem—well—you seem different.'

'I'm fine, Dee. Don't worry.' In her turn, Leila looked carefully at her friend. 'What are you so pleased about?'

Dee beamed and gave her a smacking kiss. 'Can't you guess? I'm pregnant.'

'Oh, you clever thing!' Leila gasped. 'What does Sam say?'

Dee laughed. 'He's over the moon! You'd think nobody had ever started a baby before. It's due about the middle of March.'

'You'll be leaving here soon, then?'

'Yes. Sam's decided on G.P. work, so he's given them notice at the hospital. Now he's torn between a rural practice and an inner-city one.'

'Inner-city? I know that's where good G.P.s are needed but you'd have to live there, wouldn't you? Would you like that?'

'I don't mind,' said Dee blithely. 'If it's right for Sam. it's right for me. I'm so lucky, what with him and now the baby.'

'I think Sam's pretty lucky as well,' said Leila, giving her a squeeze. 'Come on, let's have a cup of tea. What do you want, a boy or a girl?'

'Are you all right, bonnie lass?' It was Ben, at the door of the cabin as soon as she arrived. Apparently he thought that because she'd been away for a day she'd been ill.

'Oh, I'm fine, Ben. I just took a day off because I felt like a break. I don't have to work set hours like you and the lads, you see. I'm paid a fee for this job, not a wage.'

'A fee!' He was impressed. 'By, but the lads'll be surprised when I tell 'em that. We were looking for you yesterday. Shorty thought perhaps you'd like to come to the pub after work to celebrate. His missis has had a little lad.'

'Oh, I *am* glad.' Shorty was an ex-Garland man and Leila had known him since his teens. Immensely tall, with silver-blond hair and an imaginative line in cursing, he was one of her favourites. 'I'll come with you tonight, or did you all go yesterday?'

'Aye. But we can go again the day,' Ben agreed amiably. 'Shorty says they've waited seven years for this bairn so he's entitled to celebrate twice over.'

'I'll come tonight,' she promised. 'Tell the lads the drinks are on me. Is he still on the main drain?' Shorty was an expert on connecting big drainpipes and seemed to spend half his working life in trenches or holes. 'I'll go and congratulate him in a minute.'

She was standing on a chair putting up her big watercolour of the site when Pete arrived. He looked extremely uncomfortable.

'Hello, Leila. Is everything—all right? I was a bit

worried when you didn't come in yesterday.' She knew
it was as near as he could get to asking if she was
feeling any ill-effects after going to bed with a drunk.

She thought if he'd asked her that twenty-four hours
ago he might have got a different answer. 'I'm fine,
Pete. I decided to take the day off as I had a lot to do
apart from my work here.'

'Oh, I see.' If he felt relief at that he didn't show it. 'I
might not see you for coffee today. Martin Deeds is
coming to go over a few points with me.'

'Right.' She smiled casually over her shoulder.
Something about his attitude told her that she would be
seeing less of him; he was scared to death of getting
more involved with her. He little knew there was no
chance of any such thing.

She began to wonder if the whole work-force had
missed her when Jacob arrived at the cabin just before
midday. His small bright eyes showed a distinct glint of
friendliness as he presented her with a covered plate.
'Just thought you might fancy a bacon sandwich,' he
said abruptly. 'Eat it while the bacon's hot!'

Astounded, she thanked him and watched as he
marched away across the duckboards. Surely she hadn't
been promoted to his list of approved workers? She
uncovered the sandwich and groaned aloud. Two slices
of inch-thick bread with at least four rashers of crispy
bacon between. She cut off a small piece and was
amazed to find it delicious, so she made a pot of tea
and ate the whole enormous sandwich. It would do as
her lunch instead of her usual salad.

That evening after work she met the Garland men in
the local pub, wondering why she hadn't thought of
such a meeting before. Matt's ban on mixing with the
men on site had meant that she hardly spoke to them.
Shorty stood at the bar, his face one big smile, while the
others teased him about the baby and asked whether it
would be twins next time.

After a while she slipped Ben some more money and
left them, thinking that there would be several husbands
late home from work for the second time that week.

*　　*　　*

Leila hurried up Bennetts Hill after signing a pile of documents for Mr Dobbs. She'd reminded the lawyer once again that she wanted her name kept secret at all costs.

'I quite understand, Miss Garland.' She detected a faint smirk on his face and wondered just what he quite understood. 'I must point out once again that I very much doubt whether half a million will save the company. Things have deteriorated since we last met and now I hear that Mr Parnell has been offering some of his heavy equipment to the highest bidder.'

'Selling the heavy plant? But—has anyone bought it?'

'Of course not,' said Mr Dobbs with a trace of smugness. 'There is no market for it at present.'

She felt sick. The thought of Matt, tough, proud and self-reliant, hawking his surplus equipment around people who didn't want to buy it was more than she could stomach. 'I see. Still go ahead, if you please, Mr Dobbs. You're sure you won't need me again for more signatures? Good. Perhaps you'd write to me at my Edgbaston address if Mr Parnell takes up the offer?'

Thankfully she left the office; his air of disapproval irritated her intensely. Now she was acting purely on impulse. It was only two minutes' walk to the Cowper rooms, and she found the same elderly clerk on duty behind the big counter.

'Good morning. Could you possibly tell me the whereabouts of Mr Robin Cowper?'

'Certainly, Miss. Upstairs in his office.'

'Oh,' said Leila surprised. 'I see. I didn't realise he had a permanent office in the building. Could you please tell him that Miss Garland is here to see him?'

In two minutes the clerk was showing her into an office on the second floor and Rob was leaping to meet her. He was immaculate as ever, though in shirt sleeves, and his hair had been cut very short, emphasising his un-English bone structure.

'Leila! This is great! What brings you here at this unearthly hour?'

'It *is* early, Rob. I'm sorry about that. I've come to talk to you about Parnell's—the business itself.'

'Oh yes?' He was wary. 'Come and sit down, Leila.'

He led her to a buttoned leather chair and sat facing her. 'Now, what is it exactly, about Parnell's?'

'You hinted to me last week that the firm might be in difficulties, Rob. Do you know you were right? They are.'

'Of course we know.' The royal 'we', she noted. 'Iris keeps us informed of the state of all Cowper contractors. Last week she was as close as an oyster about it, but we know the set-up now.'

'What I've come to ask is this. As Parnell's are your contractors for the Bequest project, are you going to help them remain solvent?'

It wouldn't have been much of an exaggeration to say that Rob's jaw dropped; it certainly sagged. 'You don't mince your words, do you, Leila? What makes you think that we might help him?'

'The fact that he's your contractor,' she said, frowning. 'Surely it's to your benefit that he completes the job?'

'Of course it is. But it's not beyond the realms of possibility for someone else to carry on where he leaves off.'

She stared at him. 'You mean you'd contract another firm?'

'We'd have to if he went bust, wouldn't we?' He had leaned forward so that their faces were only inches apart. The dark, alert eyes were watching her carefully, and she felt faintly repelled by his alien appearance. With that haircut he looked all eyes and cheekbones. 'You needn't worry, Leila. Your fee is payable by Cowper. You're a separate entity from the builder.'

'That isn't my main concern.' It wasn't her concern at all, but she could hardly tell Rob that. 'I just thought that if you could see your way to lending him, say, half a million, it would see him through this bad patch.'

'What about you lending him some, Leila?' There was a calculating expression on his face.

She hesitated. Why not tell him? Instinct shrieked at her to say nothing about the loan. 'I haven't got that sort of money, Rob,' she said, shaking her head.

He jumped to his feet and padded restlessly round the room. 'I might as well tell you,' he said at last. 'You'll know anyway, in a few days' time. Iris has master-minded everything to do with Parnell. She's going to save the company single-handed as soon as the marriage is announced.'

Something seemed to hit Leila a sickening blow just above the waist. 'Matt's asked her to marry him?' she said slowly.

'I didn't say that. It's more a case of them reaching a mutual decision. It's not official yet. Iris doesn't want to admit that he's played hard to get.'

'Oh.' There was no point in saying more, and Rob was looking at her very oddly. 'It's bad news, isn't it, Leila?' he asked. 'You don't like it?'

She shrugged. 'The company will be safe, the men kept in their jobs. And Iris is very lovely.'

'Mm. What about us, Leila?'

'Us? You and me?' She looked into his eyes and they could have belonged to a stranger. 'I'm sorry, Rob.'

He put out his hands and grabbed her wrists. 'It's him, isn't it?' he said furiously. 'It's Parnell, not the dead man. That's why you're here, begging for money. It's him you want!'

'Let go of my wrists, Rob! As a matter of fact, yes, I do like Matt—very much.' The saying of it out loud, even to Rob, gave her a twisted sort of pleasure. 'He doesn't know how I feel and I'd very much appreciate it if you didn't tell him—or Iris.' She lowered her eyes, and knew, too late, that she shouldn't have told him. 'I realise it won't come to anything, Rob. I expect in time I'll get over it.'

He pursed his lips. 'Yes. I expect you will,' he said, smiling faintly. She knew in that instant that she was free of Rob Cowper. He wasn't the man to welcome another man's reject. He bent and kissed her wrist with an odd air of finality. 'I won't say anything,' he promised quietly. 'Goodbye, Leila.'

She walked to the door. She felt chilled to the bone. 'Goodbye, Rob. Perhaps I'll see you in a few months' time at the official opening of the leisure centre.'

He had turned away from her and was staring out of the window. 'Perhaps,' he said. 'Yes, perhaps I'll be there.'

Slowly Leila walked to Colmore Row. Her knees felt stiff like those of an old, old woman. Pictures of herself and Matt jerked about in her mind ... The time he'd cuddled her after the nightmare, the way she had cleaned the gash on his chest, the tour of the sites in his helicopter, only a week ago. Fool that she was, she'd wondered if he'd taken her on that flight because he had to sell the machine and knew that she'd never yet been up in it.

For what she swore would be the last time, she recalled what had happened afterwards. She'd never seen Matt as a man to indulge in passionate interludes with any woman who happened to be handy, so all along she'd cherished the idea that it hadn't been a mere whim with him, a passing impulse, but had meant as much to him as it did to her.

She had entertained all sorts of idiotic ideas because she loved him. Now, reality had wiped them all away.

CHAPTER FOURTEEN

LEILA set out for work reluctantly the following Monday. If the day turned out to be only half as bad as Friday it would still be horrible. The pain of it had remained with her throughout the weekend. Like a sharp-toothed animal gnawing away at her heart.

After going to see Rob she had spent most of the day at the newly cleaned stretch of water, supervising the building-up of the little island and ensuring that the giant earth-movers were shaping the far bank as she'd planned it. She was in such low spirits that the men watched her uneasily and checked their usual shouting, as if in the presence of an invalid.

The weather was sultry again, and her hair was damp with perspiration under the obligatory hard hat; her cotton shirt was stained with mud and her jeans were wet from wading in the shallows beyond the protection of her wellies. She was tired and very dirty, so at four o'clock she knocked off for a while and walked back to the cabin for a glass of milk.

She could have groaned aloud at the sight of Iris just leaving her silver Porsche on the approach road. Matt wasn't around, so she might possibly have to deal with her. Evidently that was Iris's intention, because she was heading straight for the cabin, long-legged, cool, and elegant in a pink linen suit.

'Hello, Leila. I was just heading for the motorway when I realised I had half an hour to spare, so I thought I'd come to look at the site and see you as well.' She gazed around her and put a pink-tipped hand to her forehead. 'Lord—what a *mess*! How can you stand it? And Matt has been telling me that everything's in apple-pie order here. But your office is lovely—the only spot of colour on the whole site.'

Her words had the effect of putting Leila on the defensive. The fact that Iris was going to marry the boss was no reason to speak disparagingly about his site. 'They always look like this in the early stages, Iris. Matt's quite right—it really is in apple-pie order. Come in and have a cold drink.'

Gracefully Iris sank into an armchair and accepted a fruit juice, then said: 'I take it you haven't seen Matt today?'

'No. He may have called in briefly but if so I didn't see him. Why?'

Iris leaned forward confidentially. 'It's not being announced for a few days, but I thought he might have told you. We're going to be married.'

Thank God she'd been forewarned by Rob. 'Oh, Iris. How lovely!' Surely the words carried no conviction? 'I do hope you'll both be very happy. I must congratulate Matt when I next see him.'

Perhaps it had sounded convincing, because Iris said, 'I thought you'd be pleased, Leila. Matt and I have known each other well for quite a while, you know.'

'I thought perhaps you had.' She looked at the other woman's long, well-kept hands. There was no engagement ring. 'You say it's not official yet?'

'No. We're having a big family party next Wednesday, and we hope to announce it them. Has Rob asked you to come?'

Leila shook her head. 'No. I don't think Rob and I will be seeing much of each other in future.' She sought for a feasible reason. 'We don't make much of an impact on each other.'

'Really?' Iris looked round the well-appointed little office. 'I should have thought you'd made quite an impact on him at the time he ordered this place for you.'

'Oh. Well—it is lovely, I agree. But it's a bit luxurious, you know, for a building-site.'

Iris laughed. 'That's Rob. All or nothing. Still, I think you need some compensation for working in all this mud and filth.'

'I don't mind,' Leila protested. 'My father was a builder, so I've always been used to it.' She looked at the young woman opposite her and told herself bleakly that Matt could do far worse. Iris was beautiful, she was pleasant and very intelligent, she had money, she had connections, and—most important of all—she loved him.

'How about your wedding?' she asked gently. 'Have you fixed a date yet?'

'No. But I imagine either late next month or early October, something like that.'

'Oh, so soon?' She wished Iris would leave; now, at once, because she couldn't keep up this show of friendly interest for much longer.

As if reading her mind, Iris stood up. 'I'd better be on my way. It's been lovely seeing you. Don't work too hard—oh!' She leaned across the cluttered workbench to look out of the window. 'Look—there's Matt!'

Before Leila could prevent her she was at the door waving and beckoning to him. 'You can congratulate him while I'm here,' she said, smiling. 'How lovely!'

Matt came across and stood inside the doorway. He was wearing a dark suit with a shirt and tie as if he'd been into the city on business, and looked his usual forceful self. 'Iris—what are you doing here?' He bent and kissed her cheek, then glanced at Leila. His eyes were calm and, she thought, quite uncaring. 'Leila,' he said, with a nod.

She held out her hand. 'Iris has just given me advance notice of your news,' she said warmly. 'Congratulations, Matt.'

He enclosed her hand briefly in his. 'Thanks.' She saw his eyes flick across to Iris's cool beauty, and briefly back to her own sweat-stained, bedraggled form. Why didn't they *go*, for heaven's sake?

'Come on, Matt.' Iris smiled up at him. 'Leila's busy, I can see that.'

Together they walked across to his caravan, and she saw Matt's hand placed lightly behind Iris's pink-clad waist. She was reminded forcibly of the time they'd left the dance-floor together at the barbecue, and she sat down weakly, her legs suddenly reluctant to bear her weight.

After a few moments she put her hat back on and

headed out to the lake again. Perhaps it was as well that she had plenty to occupy her.

The weekend had seemed endless, with hours of heavy rain. She'd tried not to think of Matt, but her mind obstinately re-examined their times together, repeated their conversations, so that she went out in the pouring rain and walked the tree-lined streets, the park, the local shops, until she was exhausted. Her last thought before falling asleep on Sunday night had been one of utter dismay; suppose they asked her to the wedding?

The one redeeming feature of Monday morning was that it was cooler. A fresh breeze blew across the site, bringing the sound of diesel trains from far away along the line. Pete waved to her as she clumped past the foundations of the swimming pools on her way to the lake. 'Morning, Leila. I'll come and see you at afternoon break if you have a minute to spare.'

'Yes. See you then.' Was it her imagination or did he seem a bit happier? Whatever he wanted to see her about, she hoped it wouldn't involve a long session of providing a listening ear. She couldn't face it today.

The noise of a pump drew her towards the pit for the main drain. Such deep holes had always fascinated her; she could remember being forcibly banned from going anywhere near them when she was eight or nine years old. This one was particularly good. About twenty feet deep and eight feet square, its straight sides were shored up by stout timbers and its base was ready for the main storm drain to be connected to the big outlet from the deep end of the swimming baths. Yellow water swilled beneath the labouring pump and Shorty was down there, as usual.

'How's the baby?' she bellowed.

He looked up and grinned, his teeth flashing in a face already filthy. 'Fine, just fine,' he shouted back proudly. 'The wife says he's the biggest in the nursery.' No wonder, if he takes after his father for size, she thought, moving on.

A moment later she had to move to one side as a lorry carrying piping revved its way past her. The driver must be new, she thought, to risk getting stuck in the mud out here; most deliveries were left stacked near the gates after heavy rain, it was a wonder the stock foreman hadn't stopped him. She walked on, to be halted by a shout of rage from Pete, followed by the frenzied revving of an engine.

The lorry had slid backwards down a slight slope and its rear end was within four or five yards of the drain hole. She hesitated, about to turn back, when Ben Ford ran past her, cursing, and she realised he'd seen what was happening from the vantage point of his high cab on the crane by the lake.

She watched as the lorry moved slowly forward to safety. Then, like a slow-motion shot from a disaster movie, the tops of the boards shoring up the hole fell inwards one after the other like dominoes, and a great rush of mud and slurry followed them, leaving a hollow in the land. Spurred by sick dread she ran back, seeing the shocked uncomprehending face of the lorry driver, and hearing the short whistle blasts which were the site alarm signal.

Ben ran past her again, his face as grey as his hair, and she knew he was going back for the crane. But it would be too heavy to take near the hole—it might make even more of it collapse! She stopped short. It was a terrible sight, the timbers criss-crossed and spiking upwards, with earth heaped on top and sliding down through the spaces.

Pete was there sending men scurrying back and forth and bending forward to see if any sound came up from Shorty. Silence fell across the site as one by one men stopped their machines in response to the alarm. Within half a minute there was just the knocking of the little pump beneath the boards and rubble. Then, adding a last touch of horror, the rhythmic sound slowed and coughed to a halt.

Pete seemed relieved. 'He might hear us now.' He leaned forward and called, 'Shorty. Can you hear?'

A faint shout came from below and a murmur of relief went round the men. Two navvies ran up, their spades at the ready. 'Out of it,' snarled Pete. 'Don't touch anything. He's got air down there. Disturb what's above and you'll either suffocate him or bury him—or both.' He stood back and shouted. 'Listen to me! Nobody goes down. Nobody touches those boards. Where's the ropes?'

Somebody passed him coils of rope. Two men started to tie them to the tops of those boards still left in place, their movements so delicate and careful they had a ludicrous air, like two burly labourers in wellingtons taking part in a modern ballet.

'Six men over here,' ordered Pete. 'Hold these ropes and stand well back to take the strain. We've got to keep the rest of it from falling in.' Even as the men backed off there was a groan of wet timbers and a crack as the cross-stays snapped, and slowly the near-side of the hole fell in.

'Shorty!' yelled Pete. 'Can you hear me?'

From far below came the sound of coughing. 'He's alive,' said Pete. 'The boards have saved him so far.' He turned round helplessly, and Leila knew he was hoping to see Matt. The lorry-driver came up and caught at his arm. Pete turned on him and swore viciously. Terrified, the youngster scuttled away and Leila felt a stab of deep pity for him.

Two men came up with an oxygen cylinder from the accident shed and a long length of air-pipe. 'We can't get it down to him,' a watcher said in horror. 'He's had it!'

Frenziedly Leila thought back to the lay-out of the pipes at the bottom of the hole. The big storm-drain came from behind her where the access manhole was. It was the only section that had been completed.

She rushed to Pete's side. 'Leila!' he snapped. 'Get back!'

'I'll take it!' she said. 'Through the storm-drain. Pete—I'll take the air-line. From the manhole.'

'What?' The hard eyes glared across at her. 'Nobody can get through it,' he said flatly. 'It's too narrow.' Then he stared at her slender shoulders. She grabbed the end of the air-line with its face-piece and set off. 'All right! All right !' Pete was running behind her. 'Try it! Try it! The pipe can't collapse.'

She had never moved so quickly in her life. Two men wrenched up the heavy manhole cover, while she undid her shirt and tucked the face-piece inside, under her breasts. Somebody wrenched off his thick socks and pulled them on up her arms; then she went down the ladder of the manhole, the men easing the air-line after her. At the bottom she slid the pipe between her legs and went head-first into the drain.

Bile rose in her throat at what lay ahead. Blackness—except for a tiny circle of yellow. That was the other end—there must still be light in the hole! She edged her way forward, head down, using her forearms, blessing the unknown man for the protection of his thick socks. She felt her shirt rip; the skin burn from her shoulders. A moment later the denim of her jeans went and her thighs scraped the bottom of the pipe. The thought flashed through her mind that it had been made to carry storm-water, not female flesh.

It seemed an eternity but was probably only three or four minutes before she'd covered the forty-foot stretch. The exit of the pipe was half blocked with wet earth. Muddy water slopped beneath her chest and stomach, but the faint light filtering through the broken spars seemed to her like the brilliance of noon-day sun. 'Shorty,' she croaked, 'where are you?' Why hadn't she got a torch? Why hadn't anybody thought of it? Fool—how would she have carried it anyway? She eased the socks from her arms and lay still for a moment.

She made out a space about a foot high, with crossed boards forming a roof. There, his body in water, his arms weighted by earth, a thick spar of wood pressing on his chest, lay Shorty. Leila edged out of the drain and eased the air-line up between her legs. She pressed her ear against his diaphragm, she could reach no higher, and thought she heard his breathing, faint and erratic.

She moved the face-piece to his chest, then towards his mouth and nose. The faint hiss of the oxygen was like sweet music. With a gasp of thankfulness she clamped it against his nose and struggled in vain to feel for his wrist.

An ominous creaking and groaning sounded from above, and for the second time she knew fear, this time the deadly fear that she might die—there, under the broken wood and wet earth. She wished she could get back to protect her body in the drain, but realised that she would have to turn and that might bring everything down on top of them both. There was nothing for it but to keep still and wait.

Something was sifting down through the timbers, falling with a soft hiss on to her arm. Amazed, she felt it and recognised dry, sandy soil. It must be part of a lower layer of sub-soil which had stayed dry beneath the clay. She felt more sweat break out between her shoulders at the thought of being smothered, not by slurry, but by sand.

Her breathing quietened. It was silent down there. She could hear faint sounds from above. The distinctive engine-note of the giant crane. Ben was up there. What would they try to do? Winch the timbers away one by one? She moved her shoulders a fraction and felt the spar above her shift.

The knowledge that Ben was handling the crane with its big winch attachment gave her some comfort. A picture came to her mind of a much younger Ben, entertaining a twelve-year-old girl by picking up small objects on the scoop of the crane and setting them down accurately thirty yards away. She liked that picture and thought about it for a while.

She could hear the metallic sound of steel cable. That would be the winch. How were they going to do it? Pete wouldn't let anyone stand on the rubble, would he? He was good, she admitted that, but she had seen wildness in him, sensed the panic that was close to the surface. If only Matt was in charge!

Shorty stirred. She fancied she saw the whites of his eyes gleam faintly. 'It's all right, Shorty. They're getting you out,' she whispered. 'Lie still. Please lie still. Don't move, Shorty. Don't move.'

She found herself praying that nobody would shout down to her; that nobody would take it into their head to call to her along the pipe, disturbing the air. It smelt

foul and was clouded with dust, so that she felt
reluctant to breathe in case she disturbed what was
above.

A clanking could be heard overhead. She braced
herself for someone landing on the rubble above her.
Then she felt a slight vibration. Sand sifted down on the
back of her neck, and she heard the winch going. Had
they lifted a spar? She closed her eyes and listened to
the faint hiss of the oxygen. Clods of wet earth splashed
into the water around her legs. Then she heard
scraping. No—oh no! They were digging some of the
earth out. She felt her legs stiffen expectantly but
nothing came down, except a fine sifting of sand.

She felt sleepy. Sounds came to her as if from a great
distance, far fainter than the steady hiss of the air-line.
She edged a hand beneath her cheek to keep it out of
the mud. The next thing she knew was that the same
mud was lit by the brightness of daylight, and a weight
lay across her legs. She heard a familiar voice groan;
'God in Heaven!' It was Matt. She smiled placidly into
the mud. Why had she been worried when he was here?

The winch wound busily and the weight lifted from
her legs. Then she felt someone beside her. A voice that
was familiar and yet different spoke close to her ear. It
was different because it was trembling, and she knew
Matt's voice didn't tremble. 'Leila, Leila,' he was saying
urgently, 'are you all right? Speak to me!'

With a supreme effort she turned her head and saw
one hairy arm covered with mud. 'Shorty?' she asked.

'He's out. He'll be all right. Leila—tell me, where
does it hurt?'

'All over,' she said simply. What an idiotic question.
She felt his hands move carefully over her body, feeling
for injury. 'How?' she muttered. 'How——'

'Hush! Just keep still.' She felt herself lifted and held
upright, facing him, their bodies so close she could hear
distinctly the rapid thudding of his heart. 'Can you put
your arms round my neck?' he asked.

She lifted them very slowly. How odd that somebody
should have weighted them with lead. She felt an arm
clamp around her waist, and she opened her eyes to see

the sides of the pit receding beneath them. It seemed
strange to her that it was still half full of earth and
boards; she had visualised it emptied of all rubble.

Matt held her with one arm and the cable of the
winch with the other, his feet balanced on the great
hook. 'Swing away!' he called. Gently they swung
round in an arc. She glimpsed faces circling dizzily
below them and then, level with her eyes, she saw Ben
in his cab, his face tight with concentration. Her head
cleared rapidly with the rush of air, and the thought
came to her as she circled aloft, clamped to Matt's
body: 'You'll never be this close to him again.'

Then, gently, they were deposited on the ground.
Cries of relief came from the watching men. 'Well done,
Boss,' somebody called. Matt picked her up in his arms,
and for the first time she saw his face clearly. It was
yellow-grey; exactly the colour of the cement that
sloshed round day by day in the mixers. He held her to
his chest and looked down on her for an instant. To her
dismay, she saw the glint of fury in his eyes. 'Where's
the doctor?' she heard him ask. 'Send him to the
caravan.'

Her shoulders were hurting and her thighs felt raw,
but the pain didn't seem very important. Shorty was
safe and so was she. Pete came up, flushed and
breathless. 'Leila! That was——' he began.

Matt turned on him. 'Larkin, you're fired!' he said
shortly, and with that walked off towards his caravan
with Leila in his arms, a white-coated doctor
scrambling behind them.

She thought it was time she said something. 'Matt,'
she croaked. 'Matt, put me down. I think I can walk.'

He ignored her completely and called something over
his shoulder to the doctor. She saw an ambulance
waiting by the gate—surely it wasn't for her? She
twisted in his arms but he was going up the steps and a
moment later she was laid gently on his bed.

The doctor came in. He was young and very thin.
'She'll have to be cleaned up,' he said. 'My God—what
a mess!' He examined her for fractures and sprains,
took her pulse, sounded her chest, looked into her eyes.

He stood up. 'You're a lucky girl,' he said, quite as if he himself was an old fogey of seventy. 'Under this disgusting muck you're all right, apart from a few bruises and the grazes on your thighs and shoulders.'

Matt stood there watching, as if young women with half their clothes torn from their backs were regular out-patients and the caravan their clinic. The doctor turned to him. 'She doesn't need the ambulance. It can take me back. Clean her up, especially the grazes, and you can put these on.' He took sealed dressings from his bag. 'If you're in doubt about whether you've got the dirt out run her down to casualty in an hour or two.'

He looked at Leila. 'Tetanus jabs up to date? Good. Rest for a couple of hours, then go home and have a day or two off work.' Matt saw him out, and spoke quietly to the group of men who were waiting by the door. He came back inside and the two of them were alone.

Leila's one aim was to get away. She didn't like the way he was staring at her. But first she had things to say. 'Thanks for getting me out,' she said quietly.

'Getting you out!' he repeated, his voice rising. 'Getting you out? If you hadn't gone down I wouldn't have *needed* to get you out.'

She gasped at him and fury mounted inside her, red-hot. 'You ungrateful clod!' she gasped. 'Shorty might have been dying. You might have had a corpse down your main drain!'

'I might have had two!' he replied fiercely. 'Can't you see woman, that you could have been killed?'

She felt her lower lip tremble. It wobbled up and down quite independently. She'd read about lips trembling but until that moment hadn't known that it was something you couldn't prevent. All her anger was gone, as quickly as it came. 'But—Shorty's wife's just had a baby boy,' she protested weakly. Then she burst into tears. She put her hands up to her face and found it stiff with dried mud. 'I want to go home,' she sobbed. 'I'm not staying here to be shouted at!'

He stood quite still, then he came and sat on the bed

in front of her. Deliberately he put one hand behind her
waist and the other behind her shoulders. Her shirt was
ripped and she could feel his hands, hard and warm on
her bare back. Then he kissed her on the mouth. There
was so much dirt and mud between them that she felt
grit grind against her teeth. 'Ow!' she gulped, sniffling.

'Leila Garland—I love you!' he said. 'Do you hear
that? I'm a pig and a brute to be angry with you and
make you cry, but I saw the hole collapse as I came
along the motorway, and when I got here and found
you'd gone down through the storm-drain I was nearly
demented. If I hadn't been faced with getting you out
alive, I'd have strangled Larkin there and then for
letting you do it!'

She stared at him. 'But—you're marrying Iris,' she
said slowly.

'No, I'm not. I've got a lot to say to you, Leila, but
first I must get you cleaned up. Come on.'
Dumbfounded, she let herself be carried to the shower.
'It's just as well I had this place plumbed in to the
mains,' he said ruefully. 'It's going to take an awful lot
of water to get you clean!'

With infinite tenderness he bent and removed her
wellies and socks. Then he took off what was left of her
shirt, but hesitated at the zip of her jeans. She nodded,
so he slipped the fastener down and gently eased them
over her sore thighs.

He turned away to adjust the water temperature and
she stood there shivering; partly from reaction and
partly from amazement that Matt was undressing her
and putting her under his shower, and had just told her
how he loved her.

She stepped under the warm jet of water and
removed her grubby bra and briefs. The water fell on
her bruised and filthy flesh with blissful warmth. She
was astonished at the amount of earth and mud being
swirled away down the drain.

Moments later she turned off the shower. Matt was
waiting with a big towel. He wrapped it round her and
very carefully dabbed her dry, still in the calm
impersonal manner that recalled their first meeting. He

stood back and handed her another towel. 'Wrap this round you for now,' he said, 'so that I can get at your cuts and bruises.' She did so, tucking the top in like a sarong, then he took his own towelling robe and put it across her shoulders. It was so big on her it touched her ankles. She saw him smile at that and her heart somersaulted just once, then went back to its rapid, even beat.

Apparently reluctant to let her walk so much as a step, he carried her out to the settee, propping pillows and cushions behind her. 'I'll have to clean myself up before I can deal with you,' he said. He gave her a comb and was gone.

Bemused, she towelled her hair again and combed it through. She had never known it could be such bliss merely to be clean. And then she waited.

He came out wearing denims and a cotton shirt, his hair still wet and his face back to its normal colour at last. 'First I'll deal with your dressings.' He brought water, antiseptic and swabs, and with care and the utmost delicacy tackled each golden-skinned thigh and then each shoulder. 'They're all clean,' he announced. 'No need to take you to the hospital. Do they hurt?'

'They sting a bit,' she admitted.

He helped her to put on the robe and she let the towel drop from beneath it. Then he stood back and looked at her, about to speak. Before he could say a word there was a knock on the door and Jacob walked in with tea for two on a tray. He stopped short at the sight of Leila and gave her a beaming smile. 'The lads is coming,' he said.

Sure enough there was a scuffling outside the door. Jacob opened it and two of the men came in. One was Ben Ford, the other a man she didn't know. Awkwardly they presented her with a huge, ungainly bunch of mixed flowers—somebody must have rushed to the shops for them at top speed. 'From the lads,' said Ben, 'on behalf of Shorty and his missis and the bairn. The doctor told us that the oxygen might have saved his life, what with his ribs being broken and all the dust he'd breathed in. Are you all right now, bonnie lass?'

She smiled at them both. 'I'm fine,' she said gently. 'Tell the lads thanks.'

They backed out, looking relieved, and Jacob followed them. At the door he turned. 'Drink that tea while it's hot,' he said sternly.

'Matt, was Shorty badly injured?' she asked. 'He didn't look too good down the hole.'

'I think one of his legs was mashed up a bit, and a few ribs broken.'

'You *think*! Don't you *know*?'

'I wasn't paying much attention,' he said, smiling slightly. 'I had other things on my mind. I only got him out first because I couldn't reach you until I'd moved him.' He sat on the settee and took both her hands in his. 'Leila,' he said quietly, 'was it you who offered me the loan?'

'What?' It was the last thing she'd expected to hear. 'Oh,' she said, dismayed. 'I impressed on Mr Dobbs that you weren't to be told.'

'I wasn't told. I guessed. I'm right, then?'

'Yes, what made you think it was me?'

'I was at the office when the letter arrived this morning. I couldn't imagine who was likely to offer me half a million without interest. Then I realised it was the sort of thing that a woman I know would do. A woman who takes on a difficult job when she doesn't even need to work, and in spite of opposition makes a success of it. A woman who has nightmares because a man she didn't love was drowned and she imagines she was to blame. A woman who goes to bed with another man because she's sorry for him. I just knew it was you, that's all. I was on my way to see you about it when I saw the hole fall in.'

She said urgently: 'Matt—I didn't sleep with Pete, although he wanted to because he was drunk. He passed out on my bed, and in the morning I let him think we'd slept together. It seemed the right thing to do at the time.'

He shook his head. 'Leila, I've got an awful lot of apologising to do, haven't I? I was jealous as hell, you see, just as I was jealous of Rob Cowper when I said what I did at the barbecue.' He looked down at their interlocked hands. 'I know you don't feel the same as I do but I shall go mad if I don't say that I fell in love with you as I sat and watched you while you slept on the beach of that little coral island. When I saw the card you'd left at the beach-house I had the crazy idea that perhaps you felt the same. So I followed you home. I wanted to explain about the takeover, and I desperately wanted to see you again.'

He laid one finger against her lips as she started to speak, and then looked deep into her eyes. 'You must wonder why I didn't say anything before now. I couldn't compete with a dead man, Leila. I thought you still loved Lance so I resolved to give you time to forget him without being pestered by me. I couldn't keep to that resolve after we'd had the flight in the helicopter, though. That lapse on my part was solely because I couldn't resist you any longer.

'But already things were going wrong with the firm. I badly needed an injection of ready cash to keep paying the wages. I wasn't bankrupt but I hated all the putting and taking, all the asking for credit, and I didn't want you to know about it. In the end things were so bad I went round to your flat to see if you could loan me any capital. You know what happened; not only did I believe you'd slept with Pete—forgive me for that, Leila—you told me you hadn't loved Lance. I'd left you alone for months solely because of that, and there'd been no need.

'I went back to square one—to Iris. We'd been close in the past, but always in a lighthearted way. I knew nothing of her ideas on marriage until a few weeks ago. I'd put her off because I wanted you, then I found out you weren't interested. But I would never, ever, have contemplated marriage if she hadn't made it a condition of saving the firm.'

At last she managed a question. 'Didn't you find it distasteful that she was more or less forcing you to marry her?'

'Of course. But I was faced with laying men off, even putting some of them on the dole. A million would have cleared me, but I couldn't get it except through Iris. And I'd told you I could guarantee that the Garland men would be kept in work until the current contracts were completed.'

She bit her lip. Yes—he'd told her that—when she badgered him about the future, months before. He was gripping her hands so tightly now that she squeaked in pain, and he released them, kissing each finger in apology. Then he stared at them as if he'd never seen a woman's hand before.

'Matt Parnell,' she said deliberately. 'If you'll stop your explanations for a minute and let me speak. I want to tell you I love you. I first realised it at that awful barbecue. Will you kiss me again? It might be better without the mud and grit.'

And it was better. It was noon in a caravan in the Midlands, but it seemed to Leila that when they kissed the stars wheeled dizzily in the galaxies and the planets changed their courses. He held her tenderly, though. 'I can't do justice to you when you're bruised all over and covered in antiseptic dressings,' he said, then kissed her eyes and her still-damp hair before returning to her mouth. Jacob's cup of tea went cold, but neither of them noticed.

'Matt,' she said after a while. 'Matt—half a million isn't enough, is it?'

By this time she was on his knee, the robe falling open and her raw-fleshed thighs bare. 'Not quite,' he admitted. 'It's enough to save me closing one of the sites, though. I've sold the helicopter, I've sold some of the heavy plant and I've sold the house—my mother has gone to my sister's for a while.' He lifted his hand from the silky skin above her breast, and waved a brawny arm at the caravan. 'This will have to be my home until I'm solvent again.'

After a moment he pulled the robe together and covered her shoulders. 'I don't know when I can pay you back, you know.'

'It doesn't matter,' she said simply. 'I can scrape up another thirty thousand from my other accounts if it will help. I can live on the fee from Cowpers.'

'You know I can't ask you to marry me? I won't ask you to take my name when I'm up to my eyes in debt.'

'In that case,' she declared, 'I'll have to ask you, won't I? Will you marry me, Matt? We can live in the flat at weekends and here in the caravan during the week.'

'You'll have to talk me into that,' he said doubtfully, and they both found that very funny, and laughed uproariously.

'And the wedding will have to be soon,' she added, 'before Dee gets too pregnant to be my matron of honour.'

'When I'm solvent again, do you want to go back to Hawaii?' he asked gently.

Leila shook her head. 'No. Never. I began to recover from Lance's death when I met you there, Matt. It was you who started the cure, that day when you lifted me out of the sea. I don't ever want to go back there, but when we have some money perhaps we can find another uninhabited coral island in the Pacific.'

'Yes, please,' he said laughing. 'And you can wear a muu-muu—or better still, nothing at all.'

Leila was laughing again. It seemed that she could laugh now, without a care in the world. Then she sobered. 'Matt—you won't really fire Pete, will you?'

His jaw tightened in the way she knew well. 'Matt,' she said urgently. 'You won't, will you?'

'I won't fire him,' he conceded reluctantly. 'I'll transfer him to the by-pass site. That'll teach him not to let the woman I love go crawling through drain-pipes twenty feet below ground.'

She put her head on his chest and felt the muscles hard against her. 'I've got lots more to tell you,' she said. 'Lots more to explain.'

'Later,' he murmured, his hands big but very gentle on her bruises.

It was some time before she remembered the flowers. 'I'll have to put them in water,' she said, and leaned away from him to touch them. They tumbled over the low table in a riot of colour and fragrance.

'Look, the men must have bought a bunch of everything in the shop,' she said softly. 'Sweet peas, dahlias, roses, lilies, carnations, freesia, montbretia. Aren't they lovely?'

But Matt was looking at her, not the flowers. 'Come here, Capability Rose,' he said.

ROMANCE

Variety is the spice of romance

Each month, Mills & Boon publish new romances. New stories about people falling in love. A world of variety in romance — from the best writers in the romantic world. Choose from these titles in November.

RETURN TO WALLABY CREEK Kerry Allyne
PILLOW PORTRAITS Rosemary Carter
THE DRIFTWOOD DRAGON Ann Charlton
TO CAGE A WHIRLWIND Jane Donnelly
A MAN WORTH KNOWING Alison Fraser
INJURED INNOCENT Penny Jordan
TOUCH NOT MY HEART Leigh Michaels
SWEET AS MY REVENGE Susan Napier
SOUTH SEAS AFFAIR Kay Thorpe
DANGER ZONE Madeleine Ker
*****THE GARLAND GIRL** Liza Manning
*****MacBRIDE OF TORDARROCH** Essie Summers

On sale where you buy paperbacks. If you require further information or have any difficulty obtaining them, write to: Mills & Boon Reader Service, PO Box 236, Thornton Road, Croydon, Surrey CR9 3RU, England.

*These two titles are available *only* from Mills & Boon Reader Service.

Mills & Boon the rose of romance